The smell of blood had gotten the jaguar's attention

The Executioner turned slowly as the cat circled him, never quite letting itself be seen by its intended prey. Bolan's grip on the tire iron tightened as he swung it, trying to loosen his protesting muscles.

"Walk away, pal," Bolan said. "Go look for dinner elsewhere."

The only reply he got was the sound of the animal moving through the brush. He caught the flash of a tail out of the corner of his eye. Green eyes met his and Bolan froze. He was very aware of his blood dripping onto the thirsty soil, and of the pounding of his heart.

Bolan let the tire iron slide through his fingers until he was gripping the end. He'd get one swing, just one. "So it had better be good, right?"

The jaguar snarled.

"Come on then. You want me? I'm not going anywhere."

The jaguar paused, then its muscles bunched and its tail went rigid. Bolan tensed. The cat sprang.

And the Executioner—his body honed into a weapon second-to-none—lunged to meet it.

MACK BOLAN ®

The Executioner

The Don Pendleton's
Executioner®

BORDER OFFENSIVE

A GOLD EAGLE BOOK FROM

W❂RLDWIDE®

TORONTO • NEW YORK • LONDON
AMSTERDAM • PARIS • SYDNEY • HAMBURG
STOCKHOLM • ATHENS • TOKYO • MILAN
MADRID • WARSAW • BUDAPEST • AUCKLAND

Recycling programs
for this product may
not exist in your area.

First edition November 2012

ISBN-13: 978-0-373-64408-7

Special thanks and acknowledgment to
Joshua Reynolds for his contribution to this work.

BORDER OFFENSIVE

Printed in U.S.A.

This is not a battle between the United States of America and terrorism, but between the free and democratic world and terrorism.

> —Tony Blair,
> British Prime Minister

There are no borders for terrorism—no lines it won't cross. But wherever innocent lives are threatened, I will go there and wage my war. Whether it's here at home or on soils abroad, I will fight strong.

> —Mack Bolan

THE
MACK BOLAN
LEGEND

Nothing less than a war could have fashioned the destiny of the man called Mack Bolan. Bolan earned the Executioner title in the jungle hell of Vietnam.

But this soldier also wore another name—Sergeant Mercy. He was so tagged because of the compassion he showed to wounded comrades-in-arms and Vietnamese civilians.

Mack Bolan's second tour of duty ended prematurely when he was given emergency leave to return home and bury his family, victims of the Mob. Then he declared a one-man war against the Mafia.

He confronted the Families head-on from coast to coast, and soon a hope of victory began to appear. But Bolan had broken society's every rule. That same society started gunning for this elusive warrior—to no avail.

So Bolan was offered amnesty to work within the system against terrorism. This time, as an employee of Uncle Sam, Bolan became Colonel John Phoenix. With a command center at Stony Man Farm in Virginia, he and his new allies—Able Team and Phoenix Force—waged relentless war on a new adversary: the KGB.

But when his one true love, April Rose, died at the hands of the Soviet terror machine, Bolan severed all ties with Establishment authority.

Now, after a lengthy lone-wolf struggle and much soul-searching, the Executioner has agreed to enter an "arm's-length" alliance with his government once more, reserving the right to pursue personal missions in his Everlasting War.

1

The Mexican border

The truck was military surplus, but any insignia hinting at its origins had long since faded beneath the glare of the Mexican sun. Inside the truck, beneath a reinforced tarp, rested a minor, if profitable, amount of death in posse—black tar heroin. On top of the truck, a substantially larger amount of death in esse clung to the tarp, pressing his long frame as flat as it could go. Mack Bolan blinked, trying to eject the grit from his eyes, and shifted his weight for the hundredth time in as many minutes.

It had been the task of moments getting on the truck, but the ride had been a test to his patience. The heat, the dust and the uncomfortable realities of his position were wearing down his normally stoic outlook about such things. His skin itched with dirt beneath his fatigues, and the body armor felt more and more constrictive as time wore on. He had taken numerous wounds in his long and bloody war—knives, bullets and bombs had each taken a ferryman's toll from his flesh at some point. At this moment, it seemed as if he could feel every single one of those old wounds.

Bolan bobbed his head, risking a glance at his surroundings. Buildings swept past at a lazy speed. Clapboard affairs with broken, filthy windows and signs that were no longer legible.

In other words, perfect.

A dead-end town, situated on the edge of the Sonoran Desert, caught between national boundaries. There were a hundred just like it scattered along the length of the United States' southern border—invisible, forgotten places. Some inhabited, others not, but all perfect places to do business for drug traffickers of either nationality. Like leaks in a levee, they excreted trickles of narcotics from Mexico into Texas, Arizona and California.

Bolan had been tracking the current shipment for days, hoping to plug this particular leak. He'd taken out a poppy field in Sinaloa earlier in the week, and then caught up with the shipment as it approached the Arizona border. Getting onto the truck had been interesting and had used up his quota of luck for the week. From here on out, he was playing it careful.

The truck rumbled over a pothole and Bolan gritted his teeth as he was rattled down to his bones. He tried to stretch, to work out the kinks in his limbs, knowing he'd need every iota of agility in the coming minutes. When you were dealing with a bullet, even a fraction of an inch could be a useful distance, and the difference between life and death.

According to his sources, there shouldn't be more than a dozen men all told at the rendezvous, but that was plenty. The odds were always the same once you crept up into double digits—namely, bad.

He smiled, baring his teeth. Bad odds only meant that he'd have to work fast to even them. And he was in the mood for "fast."

The truck gave a depressed growl as it came to a halt behind a two-story building that had seen better decades. Voices, speaking Spanish and English in equal measure, rose to audibility. Bolan tensed and prepared to make his move. He pushed himself up an inch, balancing on the struts holding up the tarp, and switched his grip on the Heckler & Koch UMP-45 strapped across his chest. There was a van parked nearby. It had once been white, but presently it was the color of nicotine, and it was occupied. Bolan counted eight heads, plus the man sitting in the van. The odds were better than he'd thought.

The van door slammed. "It's about damn time, Ernesto. I got places to be."

Bolan pulled himself slowly toward the edge of the truck facing away from the voices.

"Oh? Better places than this, Jorge?" someone—Ernesto, Bolan assumed—said. "I feel hurt. Here, in the heart."

"You have a heart?"

"Well, it's not mine." Laughter. Bolan hunched, rising into a slight crouch. His finger tapped the trigger guard of the submachine gun.

"Yeah, that's funny," Jorge said in a voice that implied it wasn't. "Look, get the stuff loaded. I got to go."

"Something I should know about?" Ernesto said before barking orders in Spanish. Bolan heard the tailgate of the truck come open. Metal scraped against metal.

"Sweets needs drivers."

The truck sank slightly as someone—several someones—climbed aboard. Bolan took a breath and gripped the end of a wire sticking out of the tarp. Earlier, while the truck was in motion, he'd used the KA-BAR knife strapped to his leg to cut a thin hole in the tarp. From there, he'd attached an M-18 smoke grenade—its pull ring connected to the wire in his hand—to the inside of the tarp with a strip of nonreflective tape. The men sitting in the back hadn't noticed. They would in a minute.

Gripping the wire, he prepared to roll off the edge of the roof.

"Drivers? For what? He outsourcing now?" Ernesto said.

"Not quite. He's got a hundred units need to be over the border yesterday."

Bolan froze. Units? Did they mean weapons? Other than drugs, weapons were often smuggled to inner city gangs in the Southwest. He listened.

"A hundred. Huh. That's more than usual." Ernesto grunted.

"That's what I said. Know what he said?"

"Sweets?"

"Yeah. He said, money can roll back the most stubborn of tides," Jorge said.

Ernesto snorted and said, "Maybe my English is not so good. That makes no sense."

"I speak English perfectly. It makes no damn sense to me, either. Goddamn Zen cowboy shit."

The truck bounced under Bolan as the merchandise was moved out. He had to act while the majority of the smugglers were in the truck, but he wanted to hear the rest of the conversation.

Decisions, decisions.

Moments later, his choice was made for him. He heard a muffled question in Spanish. Something jostled the wire in his hand. Bolan moved instantly. He rolled off the edge of the truck, hauling the wire with him. Something went *ping* even as he hit the ground.

The gas canister hit the bed of the truck and vomited dark smoke with a serpentine hiss. Cries of alarm echoed from within. Bolan let off a burst through the tarp, then rose into a crouch and swung around the edge of the tailgate, the UMP-45 cradled in both hands. A smuggler, tall, dressed in surplus fatigues and wild-eyed, half fell out of the truck. Bolan pulled back on the trigger, sending the man's body jerking and whirling away.

"Shit! What—" A tall Mexican that Bolan figured was Ernesto dug for a large pistol holstered beneath one arm. He was dressed well, in a thin suit, his dark shirt open nearly to his navel. Bolan caught sight of a gaudy tattoo as the smuggler dived behind the other side of the truck.

A machine gun chattered and tore through the tarp, forcing Bolan to dodge it. The Executioner moved with lethal grace, springing to his feet and sliding around the back of the truck. Smoke boiled out of it, and he let off a second short burst into the interior. He spun on his heel, his weapon snarling. Another smuggler was punched backward, a spray of red arcing from his face and chest. The UMP clicked on empty. Bolan reached for another clip.

A man lunged at him, machete whistling through the air. Bolan let the UMP fall to dangle from its strap, and stepped aside, swatting the blade of the machete with the flat of his hand. He slapped the blade down to the ground and swept its owner's feet out from under him. As the smuggler fell, Bolan kicked the machete away.

Colored smoke hung thick on the air, and he could hear the scratch of rubber soles on dirt. Bolan jabbed his opponent quickly in the face, then, as the smuggler reeled back, clutching at his nose, the big American rammed his fist into the man's throat. Cartilage crumpled and the man collapsed, gagging. Bolan swept up the machete and reversed it with a twirl of his wrist, driving it down into the smuggler's skull with a wet crunch.

Bullets plucked at the ground at his feet and he sprinted forward, toward the van. The owner—Jorge—was a light-skinned man, built stocky, and he backpedaled, hands up, despite the pistol on his hip, as Bolan thundered toward him out of the smoke.

"Wait, wait, wait—" he shouted as Bolan slammed into him, shoulder first. They went down together, but only Bolan came up. He grabbed Jorge's shirtfront and slung him bodily behind the van.

"Damn it, wait!" Jorge yelped. Bolan knocked him sprawling and joined him behind the van.

"You keep quiet. Maybe you'll live through this."

Ernesto and two men, both armed with AK-47s, moved forward out of the smoke, looking around wildly. Bolan pressed his foot to Jorge's throat and twisted around the edge of the van, bringing his weapon up even as he slammed a full magazine home.

"Hey! *Gringo,* you going to—" Ernesto began.

The UMP burped. Ernesto screeched, and his pistol discharged as he toppled. His companions fell more quietly. Bolan waited a minute, then two. He relaxed slightly. No movement from the truck.

All in all, it had taken only a few minutes. It had been a textbook takedown. Bolan slid his foot away from Jorge's throat, but kept his weapon aimed at the man.

"Good afternoon. Jorge, was it?" Bolan said, squatting and yanking the pistol from the man's holster. He tossed it aside.

"Jimmy-Jorge James actually," the man croaked. "Who the hell are you?"

"Interesting name," Bolan said, ignoring the question.

"Blame my parents," Jimmy-Jorge James said. "So, you kill Ernesto?"

"Yes."

"Crap. I'm going to reach into my pants, get something you probably need to see." James waited for Bolan's nod, then reached into his trousers and pulled out a bill folder. He tossed it to Bolan. Bolan flipped it open and quirked an eyebrow in surprise.

"You're border patrol?"

"That's what it says on the badge, *hombre.*" James rubbed the back of his neck. "And you, my friend, just potentially blew two very important federal operations! Now, who the hell are you?"

"I'll ask the questions. What were you doing here?" Bolan said.

"I was running a sting operation on poor old Ernesto there. Got a problem with that?" James said belligerently. He made to get up, but Bolan motioned for him to stay down.

"Not yet," he said pleasantly. "Not until I know you are who you say you are. And that you were doing what you claim you were doing."

"Yes, because I'm the untrustworthy one here," James said harshly, indicating the bodies all around.

"A little paranoia is good for the soul," Bolan said calmly. He eyed the badge, looking for telltale signs that it was a fake. Finding nothing to indicate that it was anything other than what it seemed, he let the UMP fall to dangle from his shoulder and reached up to detach the satellite phone from his harness. It would be a simple enough matter to have someone check out the badge number and the identification.

James, however, didn't seem inclined to wait. As Bolan dialed, the younger man suddenly rolled toward his pistol with the speed of a rattlesnake on the strike. As Bolan cursed and brought his weapon up one-handed, James scooped up the pistol and twisted around, sighting down the barrel.

Bolan ducked to the side even as Jorge fired. Behind him, someone screamed. Bolan spun, and his UMP hummed as he let off a burst into Ernesto's already sagging body. James's bullet had torn a neat, round hole in the smuggler's cranium, sending him into the darkness just ahead of Bolan's own burst. Lowering his smoking weapon, Bolan turned back to James, who smiled at him weakly.

"Sorry. Instinct, man," James said, letting his pistol spin around his trigger finger until the butt was facing Bolan. "You can have it back now."

"Keep it," Bolan said simply.

2

"He's legit," Hal Brognola said, his voice echoing oddly through the receiver of the satellite phone. "He's been with the United States Border Patrol for ten years, straight out of college. He's a good one, Striker."

"He mentioned Interpol," Bolan said.

"Seconded, recently," the big Fed said. "He and his partner."

"Partner?" Bolan looked at James, where he squatted beside Ernesto's body, going through the man's pockets. "He didn't mention a partner."

"Why would he? He doesn't know if you're legit, either, Striker," Brognola said, sounding amused. Bolan grunted. There was truth in that.

"I guess I don't have one of those faces, huh?"

"Not even close." Brognola cleared his throat. "From what I can tell, you just dropped into the middle of something that's been in play for a while, barring recent changes."

"I'm not going to like this, am I?" Bolan said.

"No, not really. It's a mess, and only going to get messier. Interpol's involved, Border Patrol wants the coyotes shut down and all the other federal agencies are screaming about being kept out of the loop. No one really knows what's going on out there."

"Including us," Bolan said.

"How is that new?" Brognola said.

"It's not," Bolan said. "Well, whatever the game is, I'm dealing myself in."

"Why did I have a feeling you'd say that?" Brognola sighed. "Look, I'll try to find out what's going on, on my end. Keep me posted on yours. Oh, and, Striker? Let's keep the property damage to a minimum until we know whose field we're playing in, okay?"

"Sure thing," Bolan said and turned off the phone. He clipped it back on his rig and started toward James. "You didn't tell me you had a partner," he said. The border patrol agent stood, clapping dirt off his pants.

"Figured if you were really who you said you were, you'd find out, Cooper." He rubbed his cheek. Bolan had given James the name of his Justice Department cover identity, Agent Matt Cooper, reasoning that it was the quickest way to get the man to trust him. So far, it seemed to have worked.

"Well, I have. Who is he?"

"He's a 'she,' actually. Her name's Amira Tanzir, with Interpol. She's working things from the back end." James watched curiously as Bolan knelt and grabbed Ernesto's legs. "What are you doing?"

"I'm moving the bodies onto the truck. Jihadists," Bolan said, dragging the body up into the truck. Clapping his hands together, he hopped down and made for another one.

"Maybe—that's the rumor at any rate," James said, rubbing his throat. "Hell, I don't know, I just go where they tell me, Cooper."

"But that's the rumor."

"Yeah," he said. Bolan looked at him as he got another body onto the truck. According to Brognola, Jimmy-Jorge James was a veteran of countless border skirmishes with smugglers of all types of cargo—including humans. He'd made his bones taking down snakehead rings in California before gravitating east to the Mexican front, and the troubles there.

Presently he was acting as a dogsbody for Interpol. Bolan

could tell that it grated on the man, and the Executioner allowed himself a quick smile. He knew that feeling well. You grew used to working alone, to following your own initiative. It made it hard to follow orders, when it became time to do so again. That was one of the reasons for his current arrangement with the Stony Man organization. That, and the fact that Bolan felt that he was simply more effective on his own. He moved the last body onto the tailgate of the truck and shut it, flipping the body onto the others.

"How long have you been under?" Bolan said, rounding the truck and sinking to his haunches. He unsheathed his KA-BAR and punctured the gas tank with one swift, economical strike. Rising to his feet, he looked at James.

"Only a few months," the young agent said. "We got word that some of the cartels were using coyotes to get pigment—"

"Pigment?" Bolan said, stepping away from the thin trail of gasoline carving a swath through the dirt of the street. "Step back."

"Black tar heroin," James said, backing up toward his van. "Are you sure about this?"

"You'd rather I leave it here?"

"I'd rather you let me call my bosses and let them come confiscate it. Have you ever heard of chain of evidence?"

"No guarantees they'd get to it before someone else did. I'd hate to have gone through all this trouble just to see this crap wind up right where it was going anyway," Bolan said, pulling a box of matches out of one of the pockets on his combat rig.

"Yeah, about that," James said. "What the hell was this about? You guys could have let us know you were planning an operation on our patch."

"No time, I'm afraid. Jihadists," Bolan said, trying to steer the conversation back on topic and away from dangerous shoals.

"Yeah, well, same shit, different angle. I got myself established as a coyote. I got some routes, made friends, that kind of thing." James leaned against the side of his van, arms crossed. "I met Sweets."

"Who's Sweets?" Bolan said, lighting a match. He dropped it and stepped back in a hurry. The tiny flame caught and zipped back along the gasoline trickle.

"Sweets is Django Sweets. Big-time king coyote. Runs people, drugs, guns, car parts, whatever you want, whichever direction you want them going in. Coyotes have sort of an informal union, if you can believe it."

Bolan could. He'd seen it again and again with various types of criminals. Someone invariably put themselves on top. "Yes," he said. When he didn't elaborate, James went on.

"Sweets put himself in the top spot a few months back. He's in slick with the cartels, and, unfortunately, it looks like he's got an in with us as well. He's been running mules—illegal migrants carrying drugs—into Tucson and such, and he's skated out of at least two sure-thing sting operations."

"So you are saying you have a leak?" Bolan said. The truck was engulfed in flames, taking the heroin and the bodies of the transporters with it.

"Worse. We think Sweets has got people covering for him. Don't know who though. We were hoping to scoop them up in the middle of all this."

"All what?" Bolan said. "All my contact knew was that it was a mess."

"Sweets was contacted a few weeks ago by a guy named Tuerto," James said.

Bolan blinked. "One-Eye?" he said, translating.

"Mr. One-Eye, actually, or at least, that's how Sweets referred to him." James shook his head. "We had no clue who he was at the time, but then we got a panicky shout-out from Interpol."

"Terrorist?"

"Worse. He's a mercenary, and a good one. His sticky fingerprints are all over a number of incidents going from one end of the world to the other." James shrugged. "At least, that's what Interpol said. And they should know, because they've been tracking him for three years."

"Your partner," Bolan said, reading between the lines. James nodded.

"Yeah, she's some hot shit, according to her bosses. Undercover work, tactical assault, all that jazz."

"And what do you make of her?" Bolan asked shrewdly. Tanzir sounded competent, if nothing else.

James was silent for a moment. Bolan could practically see the gears turning in his head. When he finally answered, he chose his words with care. "She's…intense. Tuerto's…" He trailed off. "Listen, have you ever read any Melville?"

Bolan caught his meaning instantly. "He's her white whale," he said.

James shrugged, obviously uncomfortable. "Something close to that…. She's not obsessed, but she's real focused." James made a gesture. "Tunnel vision, you know?"

"I know." Bolan felt a pang. More than one person had accused him of something similar over the years, and he couldn't say that they were entirely wrong. A small part of him was looking forward to meeting Ms. Tanzir more and more.

James looked at him. "Yeah, I bet you do," he said, not unkindly. "I only met her once, really. She wasn't happy about the situation. Nor was I, for that matter."

"I bet you weren't," Bolan said.

"Neither was her fellow," James added, chuckling.

"Fellow?" Bolan said, curious despite himself. "As in significant other?"

"Very significant," James said. "One of the head honchos of the Interpol contingent. Some French guy. Boy-howdy, that guy was not happy about her being there."

"Worried about her?"

"To be honest, I couldn't tell…it was either her, or the mission, with even odds as to which. Maybe both, for all I know."

The border patrol agent shook his head. "Guy was all hot and bothered, in a bad way, about her part in things."

"Speaking of which, if you're here, where is she? You said something about the back end?" Bolan said, trying to pull them back to the topic at hand.

James grunted. "Interpol has been helping the Mexican authorities with the cartels. They've got people on the inside just like the DEA and the Spooks."

"In my experience the cartels run a tight ship," Bolan said dubiously. "They cause leaks...they don't have them themselves."

"Normally, they do. The Interpol liaison with the Mexican government swears up and down that she hasn't been made. The cartels are bringing up a load of two-legged cargo as far as the border..."

"And she'll be coming with them," Bolan said, catching on quickly. "Just one more face in the crowd." He had to admit, privately at least, that as far as plans went, it wasn't bad. Two operatives stood a better chance at succeeding than one, especially in a situation like this, which was bound to go to hell, regardless of the people involved. "This Tuerto... They tracked him here?"

"Not just him. Mexican authorities thought they had identified at least six other terror suspects." James held up his fingers for emphasis.

"And?" Bolan prodded.

"Undercover *Federales* got a picture of Sweets meeting with somebody they think is Tuerto in Mexico City. He was arranging a job."

"And since you were already in place—"

"Two birds, one stone," James said, holding up two fingers. "I love that saying." At a look from Bolan, he sped on, his words nearly tripping over one another. "Anyway, Sweets contacted me a day ago. Said he needed drivers for a shipment, and promised equal shares, good money, no questions.

He wants me to come to a meeting in some no-account shit hole he's holed up in. I said yes."

"Then what was this?" Bolan said, gesturing toward the burning truck.

"I was keeping up appearances." James shrugged. "I figured it couldn't hurt, just in case our leak decided to dime me out. A good coyote is greedy, plus, hell, if I'm going to sacrifice my op for somebody else's. I put too much effort into finding out where Ernesto's supplies were coming from—"

"Sinaloa—I already took care of it," Bolan said almost absently. The agent looked at him, mouth open.

"You what?" he said.

"I took care of it, about a day ago." Bolan smiled. "You're welcome." James shook his head, his face a study in conflicting emotions.

"I've been looking for that damn field for almost a year now. He's been shoveling so much pigment into border runners that half of them have been dying on the ground before they get two feet into Tucson. How the hell did you—?"

"Trade secret," Bolan said, patting his weapon.

"Trade—? You know what? I don't give a good goddamn, man. I really don't. You say it's done, I figure you know what you're talking about," James said, motioning toward the burning truck for emphasis.

Bolan was silent for a moment. He examined the man in front of him. James was young, but he had the look in his eye that Bolan had come to associate with professionals of high caliber—a determination to see things done, and done right. He made his decision that instant, and hoped he wouldn't regret it.

"What now?" Bolan said.

"*Now,* he asks. Now, Agent Cooper, I try to salvage what I can," James said. "I get my ass to that meeting, do my shuck-and-jive routine, and get things moving. Hopefully my erstwhile partner is already in place, then we see how shit goes down, you dig?"

"Which means?"

"The plan was to figure out where we were going—what the destination was—and have people waiting. I'd roll them right into custody, with Tanzir riding shotgun. Then, from there, we'd wrap up the rest of them." James rubbed his temples. "It sounds a lot simpler than it is."

"You'll have to get it exactly right," Bolan said in agreement. James grinned.

"I'm good at my job, man. There's no one better."

"But you wouldn't turn down help," Bolan said.

"What?" James said, blinking.

"I'm going with you," Bolan said. Normally, Bolan would have left them to it, but there was too much riding on this, and too much dependent on all the wrong people, in Bolan's estimation. The more complex a plan, the more likely it was to go wrong at the worst moment.

If even one of Tuerto's men got through, it could be a disaster of hideous proportions. It only took one man to set off a bomb, after all.

"Whoa, hold up there, chief!" James held up his hands. "I don't think that's a good idea! You aren't exactly the subtle type." He gestured at the burning truck. "If we do it my way there's no fuss, no muss."

"But my way, they don't get near the border," Bolan said. He hefted his UMP meaningfully. The other man was quiet for a minute, and then he grinned.

"Oh, we're going to be the best of friends, Agent Cooper. I can see that right now."

3

The town, such as it was, did not exist. It was not on any map, and the roads leading into it and out of it were not paved. It was one of a hundred such towns in the Sonoran Desert that clung to the edge of the map unseen and unclaimed by either of the two nations in a position to do so.

It had no name because such places needed no name. It was simply "the town."

Tariq Ibn Tumart—also known as Tuerto—had, in his life, been to many such places the world over. They were easy enough to locate, if you knew what you were looking for.

Sitting in the passenger seat of the military-surplus jeep as it rattled and groaned its way across the desert, Tumart contemplated again the twists and trials that had brought him to this point. Money figured heavily in these ruminations, as it always did. He reached up and slid a finger beneath the eye patch covering the gaping socket of his left eye, probing for an itch that was never quite there.

"Is this it?"

Tumart didn't bother to turn around. He removed his finger from his socket and examined it carefully. Then he said, "No. This is a completely different town. I thought we could sightsee. I hear they have the world's largest saguaro cactus and I simply must see it."

"What?"

Tumart sighed. "Of course, this is it. Quiet down."

"What was that about a cactus?"

"A joke… It was just a little joke, my friend."

"You joke too much, *Berber*. We are on a holy mission."

"Forgive me, Abbas. Now, if you do not kindly shut up, *Arab*, I will shoot you and our mission—holy or otherwise—will be one man weaker." Tumart turned then, an H&K USP appearing in his hand as if by magic. He aimed the pistol in a general fashion at the man occupying the seat behind him. Abbas, a thin, long-beaked Saudi, recoiled, his dark eyes widening. Tumart smiled pleasantly and tapped the barrel of the pistol to his eye-patch in a mock-salute.

"Thank you," he said, turning back around. He allowed himself a moment of petty triumph then returned to his thoughts.

Why was he here again? Ah, yes…money, he remembered.

He smiled bitterly and glanced at the driver. Fahd, he thought his name was. He was less prone to chatter than Abbas, but with altogether worse hygiene.

"You should trim your beard," Tumart said. Fahd grunted, but kept his eyes on the desert in front of the jeep. Tumart rubbed a palm over his smooth-shaven pate, and focused on their destination.

The town was the first step in an operation designed not to cripple or destroy, but to simply spread fear. An ephemeral goal, but, considering his paymasters, Tumart wasn't surprised.

He was a good Muslim, when he thought about it, but fanatical devotion to a concept of divinity was not something he indulged in. Abbas and the others, however…

"When we get there, try to keep your mouth shut," Tumart said, looking at his companions. "These men are not of the Faithful, nor are they likely to be swayed by threats."

"I will be silent," Abbas said. "But if they seek to betray us—"

"Then they will. *Ma'sa'Allah*." Tumart idly genuflected. "My plan—"

"Our plan," Abbas said. Tumart let it pass.

"Our plan hinges on this moment. We will not get another."

"Then you had best see to its success."

"That is what you are paying me for," Tumart said.

IN THE TOWN, men watched the approaching jeep with hooded eyes. "They're here, Django," someone said. And the man known as Django Sweets tipped the frayed edge of his cowboy hat up, out of his narrow face, and grinned.

He was a rawboned individual, and, at a distance, easily mistaken for the stereotypical cowboy. He sat up, the worn-down heels of his cowboy boots snapping against the wood of the floor. He adjusted the hang of the shoulder holster he wore under his denim jacket and stepped outside the empty cantina.

"How many?" he said.

"Three." The man standing nearby turned. He sniffed and rubbed his nose. "Damn ragheads."

"Shut up," Sweets said. "Don't insult our guests, Franco. We all need this score."

"So you say," Franco said.

"So my bank balance says. Yours, too," Sweets said. "Where's Digger?"

"He's, ah, he's upstairs with that woman he brought," Franco said hesitantly. Sweets frowned.

"Go get him. I want his ass down here. He should be finished by now anyway."

"Man…" Franco had turned pale.

"Get him," Sweets snarled. "Now, Franco!" Franco bobbed his head and moved back into the cantina. Sweets watched him go, then strode out, hands stuffed in the pockets of his coat. He walked out into the middle of the street and waited as the jeep pulled to a halt a few feet away. Its engine clicked as it cooled.

Tumart stood and leaned over the windshield. "No party? No welcoming committee?"

"Figured you wanted to keep this low key," Sweets said, spreading his arms. "I got some refreshments, though."

"We do not drink," Abbas said, stepping out of the jeep. Sweets looked at him, then at Tumart.

"Means more for me, then. Leave your guns."

"But—" Abbas began to protest, his hand inching toward the Glock holstered on his hip. Fahd barked at him in Arabic, and the Saudi grimaced. Tumart snatched his pistol out of the holster before he could protest and tossed it into the back of the jeep.

"Our driver will stay here," Tumart said, handing his own weapon to Fahd. "Are there any objections, Mr. Sweets?"

"It's your dime, Mr. Tuerto," Sweets replied, using Tumart's alias. Tumart smiled.

"Excellent. I may have to add that colloquialism to my repertoire."

"This way if you please, gen'lmen." Sweets turned back to the cantina and led the two inside. "We got business to discuss."

UPSTAIRS, FRANCO APPROACHED the door to Digger's room with what he would have hastily denied as trepidation in different company. "Digger? You in there?" Franco said, knocking lightly on the door. The cantina had a second floor with four rooms, one of which had been taken over by the man called Digger earlier in the day.

Such as with all criminals, human traffickers like coyotes had a pecking order. There were those like Sweets, who had some organizational ability and charisma, and those like Franco, who kept their heads down and collected their money.

Then there were those like Digger.

His real name was Philo Sweets though no one ever called him that. He was just…Digger. Not even Grave Digger, which would have made sense given certain rumors. Just Digger. A coyote, like any other, except he was Django's baby brother and sometimes his cargo didn't make it where it was supposed to go. Then, accidents did happen and no one wanted to think about it too much. Especially not Franco. Sweets wouldn't hear a word said against Digger, and he'd buried men who had a mind to take a run at his brother. The door creaked open at the touch of Franco's knuckles. He hesitated, licking his lips. There was a smell, like spoiled meat, and the whisper of voices. "Digger?"

Bedsprings whined, followed by the sound of bare feet on wood. Franco stepped back. Digger pulled the door open. He was handsome, in a chunky way. Just a tad too much excess weight to be Hollywood pretty, but under the fat was muscle. A lot of it, packed into close to seven feet of height. He smiled childishly, his eyes unfocused.

"Hi, Franco," he said. His voice was light, like a much younger, smaller man's. There were dark stains on his cheeks.

"Digger, Sweets wants you downstairs," Franco said quickly. Digger frowned.

"I'm busy."

"Now," Franco said, trying to put some steel in his voice. Digger's lip wobbled. His fingers, where they clutched the door, were red.

"But I'm busy," he said again. "Django said I could stay up here. And I'm busy."

"Yeah, I know. But now he wants you downstairs," Franco said, trying to ignore the slow trickle of red that slithered down the surface of the door. "The ragheads are here." Digger shook his head, as if trying to clear it.

"The—" He took a breath. "Yeah, okay. I'm coming. Just need to clean up." He closed the door in Franco's face without waiting for a reply. Franco, feeling faintly ill, didn't wait for him, and started back down the stairs.

As Franco retreated, Digger closed the door and turned to survey the room. It was empty, but for a bed and a bureau and a cracked and rusting sink. And the woman, of course. There was always a woman.

But no black bird.

Digger frowned and looked at his hands. There was a crust

beneath his nails, his skin was crimson to the elbow, and his mind felt fuzzy. It was a familiar feeling. He dragged the back of his forearm across his face. "I'm sorry," he said to the woman on the bed. "I just wanted to see."

She didn't reply. Not strange, considering that she had been dead for an hour. What was left of her was hardly recognizable as the woman she had been.

Digger looked at his handiwork, and a flush of shame squirted through him. "I didn't mean to," he whined, gathering up his tools and taking them to the sink. He washed them quickly, then his hands. "I just wanted to see the black bird," he continued. "I have to see it again."

He wrapped his tools up—his knives and his hooks—and set them gently into his satchel. He gave it a fond, almost guilty pat, and began cleaning himself.

"My mother showed it to me, the first time. The black bird," he said. "It whispered things to me but I can't remember them. You understand." He glanced at the ruin on the bed. "I keep looking for it, but I can't find it." He paused. "Maybe I'm looking in the wrong place."

Cleaned and dressed, he left the room, carefully shutting the door behind him.

Downstairs, Franco took a seat at the bar as Digger came down not long after, looking bright-eyed and bushy-tailed. Sweets nodded to his brother as he led his guests inside and motioned toward a table.

At another table in the corner, two other men sat. Like Franco and Digger, they had the look of rough men. A Mossberg shotgun sat on the table in front of one. The other was spinning the cylinder on a .38. They eyed the newcomers with interest, but otherwise didn't react.

"So," Sweets said, plopping himself down in his chair once more. Tumart sat opposite him.

"So."

Sweets leaned forward. "I've talked to several of my, ah, peers. There are niblets of interest."

"Niblets?" Tumart said, amused.

"Mostly for the money." Sweets leaned back, fingers interlacing behind his head. He swung his boots up on the table, eliciting a grunt of disgust from Abbas.

"Well. That is good news. How many?" Tumart said, ignoring Abbas.

"Ten. Me, Franco there. Henshaw and Morris." As Sweets said the latter, he motioned toward the two men in the corner. "My baby brother, there. And four to arrive tomorrow."

"Ten. And ten men each." Tumart sat back. He frowned and glanced at Abbas, who nodded. "That will work, I believe." He looked back at Sweets. "Your men know what to do? What we need them to do?"

"You need us to get them boys across the border at different points, mixed in among the usual assortment of wetbacks. From there, we head into the *Yoo-nited* States proper," the man with the .38 said. He popped the cylinder closed and scratched his unshaven cheek with the barrel. "Easy peasy."

"Yes," Tumart said, looking at the speaker. The man did not inspire confidence. Still, one worked with what one had. "Fine. You'll be paid when each group reaches their destination."

"Nope," Franco said. "All up front, or we ain't going nowhere."

"You—" Abbas rose to his feet, groping for the pistol that wasn't there. Tumart grabbed his arm and pulled him back down.

"And that's why we didn't let you bring weapons," Sweets said. Tumart inclined his head.

"Wise move. No."

"No?"

"No. After." Tumart knocked on the table with his knuckles. Sweets frowned and swung his legs off the table.

"I heard you guys liked to haggle…"

"Us guys?" Tumart said.

"Ragheads," Franco supplied. Tumart glanced at him. He made a pistol with his fingers and pointed at the man.

"I am starting to dislike you."

"I'll live," Franco grunted.

"The day is yet young," Tumart said. "No dickering. The agreed-upon offer was after."

"Maybe we'd like to renegotiate," Sweets said. Tumart nodded, as if this made sense. Then, smoothly, he was up, over and onto the table before anyone could react, a leaf-shaped blade sliding from his sleeve and dropping into his palm. The tip of the blade poked Sweets's Adam's apple, eliciting a thin trickle of blood. The other coyotes reacted slowly, aiming weapons in a general fashion. Tumart ignored them.

"You should have frisked me. Negotiations are closed," Tumart said, pressing lightly.

"Maybe," Sweets said. Tumart looked down. Sweets's hand held an M-9 Parabellum pistol, and it was pressed to the other man's crotch.

"Ah," Tumart said. "Well. This is awkward."

"Yeah, you done made your point," Sweets said.

"Ha." Tumart raised the blade slightly and slid back, getting off the table. "Would you settle for half and half?"

"That seems fair."

4

Bolan watched the natural beauty of the Sonoran Desert roll past as James drove. It never failed to amaze the man known as the Executioner that the same world that could produce men like those he fought could also hold sights like this. He wouldn't go as far as to say that it was life affirming, but it was close enough for him.

"I'm surprised you didn't want to talk to your own people," Bolan said without turning around.

James started, as if deep in thought. "What?"

"About me," Bolan said, turning away from the window.

James laughed. "Yeah, that would have accomplished a lot, wouldn't it?" he said snarkily.

"I could have been anybody," Bolan said.

"You've got an honest face, my friend." The agent grinned at him, and then shrugged. "Who knows? Maybe I'm just too trusting, right?"

"Maybe," Bolan said, eyeing the man. He had pegged James right, he knew. Like Bolan, the younger man played fast and loose with proper procedure in favor of getting things done, even if it meant possibly endangering himself. It was for that very reason that Bolan had decided to deal himself in. If things went wrong, at least he would be there to play damage control and maybe keep the feisty young man alive. And if that wasn't enough…well, bravado aside, there wasn't much that the Executioner couldn't handle, one way or another. "Still, your superiors won't be happy…"

"Ah, Greaves is a good guy, but he's out of his depth," James said. "Jim Greaves, I mean, my handler. Dude's so tight he craps diamonds, you know?" He hesitated. "Not literally, mind."

"I know," Bolan said, ignoring the joke. He'd met his fair share of government desk jockeys in his time who had little understanding of how things worked in the field. He'd also met his fair share of men forced into a command position that they were supremely unqualified for. "What about the Interpol contingent?"

James made a rude noise. Bolan laughed. "That bad?" he said.

"Rittermark—or *Control*, as they call him—is as tight-assed as Greaves, but less pleasant. Stiff-faced German guy, all business. I suppose he's good at his job…otherwise, he wouldn't be in charge of this thing, would he?"

"I suppose," Bolan said. Privately, however, he wondered about that very thing. Too often, men with good connections failed upward, and this sort of assignment would be a plum for any man. "What about the other one…the French guy you mentioned."

"Right, Tanzir's guy—Chantecoq," James said. "Too cool for school, that guy. Top flight detective, with eyes like marbles."

"Sounds like he made a good impression on you," Bolan said, curious.

"Yeah…better than his boss, at any rate," James said, as if embarrassed.

"Django Sweets… What can you tell me about him?" Bolan said, changing the subject.

James cleared his throat and frowned slightly. "Like I said before, he's a big-time king coyote. Story is he was a gunman for one of the cartels for a while on the red, white and blue side of the border, then he turned smuggler. He's a cool customer, though. We brought in one of those pop-psych teams the Feebs enjoy so much and they said he was a 'high-functioning socio-path,' whatever that means."

Bolan smiled slightly at the reference to the FBI. While he knew more than a few agents—or former agents in Hal Brognola's case—he would trust with his life, the organization had its share of annoying bureaucracy the same as any other federal agency. James had obviously run afoul of it at one time or another, the same as any federal agent. "It means he's dangerous," Bolan said.

James snorted. "Oh, he is that. I didn't need some armchair psychologist to tell me that. I've known Sweets maybe a month, and it's been the longest one of my life. Not to mention most tense, too." He slapped the steering wheel with a palm as he parked the van. "He's got a mouth. He likes to talk, and he likes to poke and prod. So just play it loose, let it roll off, and don't flash him any sass. That's my advice."

"Not something I'm good at, I'm afraid," Bolan said.

"Try hard. He's rattlesnake mean, and fast on the draw. He ain't playing gunslinger, get me? Guy is the real deal."

Bolan grinned mirthlessly. "I'll do my best, Scout's honor."

"You don't strike me as the scouting type, Cooper," James said. He grimaced. "And anyway, it isn't just Django you've got to worry about. There's also Digger…"

Bolan blinked at the raw distaste evident in James's voice. "Digger? Unusual name."

"Yeah, Django's baby brother," the man said, shaking his head. "And I use the term 'baby' loosely. He's seven feet if he's an inch and he's all muscle. He looks like an elephant." James looked straight ahead, his eyes narrowed. "Django is ice, but Digger is something else entirely…he's crazy, and not in a fun, party-animal sort of way. You hear stories about him…" He shook his head again. "Anyway, he's Django's attack dog. If you make a run at Django, Digger will have his teeth in your ass before you take three steps."

"I'll bear that in mind," Bolan said. Up ahead, he caught sight of a skeletal shape slouched in the desert, like the remains of a dead dragon.

"This is it…the town with no name," James said.

"The town with no name?" Bolan said.

"That's what Sweets calls it, anyway," James said. "It used to be one of them border towns, not really Mexican or American, but catering to folks on both sides of the line. The usual stuff…guns and whores and drugs and booze. That sort of thing," James went on. He grunted. "By the Second World War, when they started tightening up on things out here, a bunch of these little towns like this got caught up in things and they were all abandoned."

"All? How many are there, exactly?" Bolan asked. He had heard about these phantom towns, but he'd never seen one before. It was like driving into a snapshot of his country's history.

"Dozens," James said. "And Sweets knows them all, believe you me. He uses them like hideouts, you know?" He shook his head slightly. "Him and Digger, they don't do well in high-population-density spots, if you get me."

Bolan did. There was a certain type of man for whom civilization, with all its benefits and burdens, was simply intolerable. Modern wolfheads, they clung to the fringes, making their way as best they could. For a while, Bolan himself might have been counted among their number, but he had never truly given up society. He simply took issue with certain aspects of it.

The van moved up slowly through the dusty streets, trailing a cloud of the same behind it, the shadows cast by the sagging, arthritic buildings crawling across its roof and windshield. But where another man might have just seen empty buildings falling into ruin, Bolan saw a hundred potential snipers' nests. He'd been in numerous towns just like this one over the years,

in Eastern Europe, Africa, Asia. They were corpse-towns—
ghoulish reminders of worse times, forgotten and lonely.

"Funny," Bolan said as he calculated angles of fire and entry
and exit points. "This Sweets is a fan of Westerns, I take it."
He plucked at the loose shirt he had changed into. His body
armor and fatigues were stowed beneath the seat, and he presently wore more appropriate garb for his cover—a loose floral-
pattern shirt and denims.

"Out here, it's practically a profession," James said, reaching across Bolan to flip open his glove compartment. Battered
paperbacks featuring faded cowboys and outlaws on the cov-
ers slid out as James dug around for something. He plucked a
rag-wrapped bundle out and tossed it into Bolan's lap. "Here,
take this."

"What is it?" Bolan said as he took the bundle. It proved to
be a stubby .38 with peeling electrical tape wrapped around
the grip. He looked at James. "I think I prefer mine, thanks,"
he said.

"Oh, I'd prefer yours, too, but nobody in our line runs looking like they're ready for war, man," James said. "Hardware
like yours attracts too much attention, you know? The knife
is fine, if a bit fancy, but that H&K and the Desert Eagle have
got to go, you dig?"

Bolan immediately understood James's point and was impressed with the man's attention to details. He popped the cylinder on the revolver, spinning it gently with his palm. It was
already loaded. He pulled a round out and bounced it on his
palm for a moment before sliding it back into place and snapping the cylinder shut. "Fine. We'll play it your way."

"There's a cubbyhole beneath your feet. It's where I keep
my badge and some other odds and ends most times. Drop
your gear in there."

Bolan found the hatch and popped it open. He blinked as
he took in the assortment of hardware revealed to him—grenades, two heavy-caliber pistols and what looked like a disas-

sembled combat shotgun, as well as a pack of MREs—Meals, Ready-to-Eat—and a satellite phone. Bolan glanced at James, who grinned sheepishly. "Man's got to be prepared out here, Cooper."

Bolan snorted and dropped his weapons into the hatch and sealed it back. "There's prepared and then there's paranoid, Agent James," Bolan said, tucking the .38 into the ratty elastic holster James had scrounged for him. It clung to his hip loosely and he wished he had thought to bring a small-caliber pistol with him. It never hurt to have a holdout piece, and at least he knew it would have been tended to by the loving hands of Stony Man Farm's resident weapons guru, John Kissinger.

"Undercover work does that to you, I'm afraid," James said. "And you can just call me Jimmy or Jorge—no formalities out here. Speaking of which…what am I calling you?"

"LaMancha," Bolan said, rifling through his memory for a suitable name. It was an old identity, and it had served him well in the early years of his war. "Frank LaMancha." He hadn't used that name in several years, but it was a good one. *Don Quixote* was a favorite of his, though the correlations between his quest and that of the Man of La Mancha's were sometimes a bit too on the nose to be entirely comfortable.

"All right," James said, nodding. "Sure you can remember that, though?"

"I think so."

"Keep It Simple, Stupid. Rule one of undercover work," James said.

"A good rule in general," Bolan said.

"All right then. You're my cousin, you need money and you're helping me out on a few runs, to see how you like it. Simple?"

"Simple," Bolan said.

"Groovy. Now, let's introduce you to the guys, shall we?" James said. He and Bolan got out of the van. The wind was blowing sand and grit through the air hard enough to sting.

Bolan shaded his eyes as they ambled toward the broken-down cantina. There were more people about than he'd expected; not just would-be undocumented workers, but also a certain class of social parasite that flocked to almost every illicit gathering Bolan had ever had the misfortune to attend… pimps, prostitutes, drug-dealers and the like.

"Oh, good, you're finally here," someone sneered as they made their way up the steps to the cantina. Bolan turned and saw a portly, middle-aged man sitting in one of the creaky chairs that littered the boardwalk around the cantina. "You ain't still on strawberry-picking time, are you?"

"Hey, Franco," James said, his distaste evident. Bolan examined the man unobtrusively. What he had taken for fat at first glance was actually muscle. Franco was short and shaped like a fireplug. Jailhouse tattoos ran up and across his bare arms and neck. A prominent swastika rested between the edge of his jaw and his ear. "Is Sweets here yet?"

"Yeah, and now that your lazy ass is here, we can get started. Time is money, greaser." Franco cocked an eye at Bolan. "Who's this guy?"

"My cousin Frank," James said.

"No shit. He's big for a beaner."

"I eat my vegetables," Bolan said mildly. He looked at James. "This isn't Sweets, I take it."

"Nope, this here is Franco, which is not his real name, but is likely one he picked out of one of them Time-Life collected histories of Second World War books," James said. "Franco, say hello to my cousin, Frank LaMancha."

"Hello, Cousin Frank," Franco said. "Why are you inflicting your august personage upon us today?" He stood, bobbing up onto the soles of his cowboy boots and flexing his wide hands. His knuckles popped audibly. Bolan sized him up at once; a petty bully, spoiling for a fight.

"He needs money, Franco. And it ain't your business," James said.

"Damn well is my business if you bringing someone new into this deal," Franco said. "I don't know him. Sweets don't know him. How do we know he ain't working for somebody?"

"Because I'm vouching for him," James said.

"Oh, well, in that case," Franco said, shrugging. Then, lightning quick, his fist jabbed out, catching James in the gut. As the border patrol agent folded over wheezing, Franco rounded on Bolan and launched a kick at his knee. Bolan blocked the blow with his palms and resisted the urge to draw his weapon. People were gathering, eager to see the fight. Franco hopped back, raising his ink-covered fists. "Good reflexes for a Mexican," he grunted.

"I'll take that as a compliment," Bolan said, sliding forward lightly. He tossed off a loose blow that Franco easily deflected and then hammered a sucker punch into the other man's kidney. Franco coughed and stumbled and Bolan circled him like a wolf, jabbing and tapping at him with featherlight strikes. Then Franco uttered a wordless cry and rushed him.

Bolan knew immediately that letting Franco get his arms around him would be a mistake. The muscles in the smaller man's arm looked like steel cables for all that his belly was soft. Bolan stepped aside at the last moment and drove his elbow into the back of Franco's neck, dropping him to the ground. The thug groaned and made to stand, but Bolan stuck a boot between his shoulder blades and shoved him down. He drew the .38 then and took aim. "Stay down," he said. "I'd hate to have to shoot a man I just met."

"I feel the same way myself," someone said over the sound of a pistol being cocked. "So how about you drop the hogleg, pal?"

5

"Your professionals are brawling in the street," Tumart said, letting the threadbare curtain twitch back in place. He turned and looked at Sweets, sprawled lazily in the small room's only chair. He seemed unconcerned by both the violence below and the glares that Abbas and Fahd were tossing his way.

"They do that. High spirits is all it is. I'll stop them in a minute," Sweets said.

"This room smells of fornication," Abbas said.

"Probably because it's a whorehouse. Or used to be," Sweets drawled. Abbas flushed and spun to face Tumart.

"He insults us!"

"He insults you," Tumart said, scratching at the corner of his empty eye socket. "My nose is not so sensitive as yours." He looked at Sweets. "I do smell blood, however."

"Blood?" Sweets said, sitting up. Tumart couldn't be sure, but he thought the coyote's face blanched slightly.

"Yes. In the room opposite ours. One of your men is staying in there, is he not?"

"Digger," Sweets said. "My brother."

"Is that his name? How unusual. Is he hurt? Ill perhaps?"

"No. Not as such," Sweets said, choosing his words with obvious care. "He's just a bit odd is all. I watch out for him now that our momma is gone to Jesus." He pushed himself to his feet and trotted to the window. "What did you ask me up here for?" he said, looking out the window.

"Have the last of your drivers arrived yet? We are on a schedule."

"They're here," Sweets said. "I just need to give them a shout and see whether they're going to bite."

"I thought that you were certain of them," Abbas said sharply.

Sweets smiled at the man. "Certain is as certain does. Don't mean nothing from one moment to the next."

"How Zen," Tumart said. "But not good enough. What if they find themselves not as certain as you have assured?"

"They will be."

"But if not?" Sweets looked at him, and that look spoke volumes. Tumart nodded. "Ah," he said. "Sentimentality is for lesser men, is that it?"

"It ain't personal. Just business," Sweets said and shrugged. "If any of them punk out, we'll divide by the number we got. We can always make room and still give your boys enough local color to blend in with."

"And by make room, you mean…"

Sweets drew his thumb across his throat in a lazy gesture. "Simple ways are the best, I find. Now, if you gentlemen will excuse me, I got a fight to break up." He left the room and Tumart closed the door behind him. He turned to look at the others.

"I believe we made the right choice," the man said.

"He is a pig," Abbas snapped. Fahd, as always, said nothing.

"Yes. But pigs are dangerous." Tumart sat on the bed and rubbed his chin. "They will just as happily eat the hand that feeds them as the food they are given. Mr. Sweets is just the same. And, I feel, his men are no different. We will counsel our brothers to maintain vigilance."

"And when they have done their job?" Abbas asked.

"Then we will slaughter our fine fat pigs," Tumart said softly. "Not with relish, but out of necessity." He sat back and closed his eye. "Now, Abbas, if you would follow Fahd's example and be silent, I intend to conserve my energy for when it becomes necessary."

"So how about you drop the hogleg, pal?"

Bolan froze. Then he tossed his pistol aside and stepped off the groaning Franco. "You've got me at a disadvantage," he said, turning around.

"On purpose, I do assure you," Sweets said, gesturing with the M-9. "Go stand over there." He kicked Franco in the side as Bolan moved. "And you, Franco, get your worthless ass up." He looked over at James. "Hi, Jorge, got yourself a running partner then, eh?"

"My cousin," the border patrol agent wheezed, rubbing the spot where Franco's punch had connected. "He needs money."

"Way of the world these days." Sweets rubbed his cheek with the pistol's barrel as he examined Bolan. For a moment, the Executioner felt as if he was being sized up by a viper about to take a bite. The feeling passed quickly, however, as Sweets turned away. "Are you vouching for him, Jorge?"

"He's my cousin," James said again.

"Like blood and water, huh?" Sweets said. He grinned. "I can dig it." He turned back to Bolan. "Django Sweets."

"Frank LaMancha."

"Pleased to meetcha," Sweets said, extending a hand. Bolan took it. Sweets had a strong grip, and his skin was like leather. He pulled Bolan close and the Executioner didn't resist. "Don't pound on no one else while you're on the clock, though. I need all my boys driveworthy," he said.

"Franco pushed him, Sweets," James said.

Sweets didn't look at him. "Don't tattle, Jorge." He released Bolan's hand and stepped back. "Y'all are the last to arrive. Get inside so we can get started." Sweets turned and ambled back into the cantina, a sullen Franco on his heels. Bolan looked at James and raised an eyebrow.

James shrugged. "That's Sweets."

"So I gathered," Bolan said. James's estimation had been right on the money, he thought. Bolan had faced many men, and he recognized a nasty customer when he saw one. Sweets wasn't an especially smart man, or even a vicious one, but he was just enough of both to be intimidating to the men who followed him. Regardless, Bolan made a mental note to never let Sweets get behind him again.

Inside the cantina were nine more men, counting Sweets and Franco. They were a grab bag of ethnicities and accents, but all had the same starving-wolf look in their eyes. They were hard men, and devoted to their greed. They sat around the few tables in pairs or trios, chatting softly. James led Bolan to a table with two other men. The latter's conversation stopped as Bolan and James sat down.

"Henshaw, Eddie," James said, nodding to each man in turn. Henshaw was a slim man, with eyes like a weasel and a .38, similar to the one Bolan carried, holstered under one sweat-stained armpit. Eddie was heavier, though he looked to be less affected by the heat. He grinned jovially at Bolan and shoved a pair of twenty-dollar bills at him.

"Here's your cut, Cousin Frank," he said.

"My cut?"

"I put a C-note on you to clean Franco's fat ass. Figure it's only fair we go sixty-forty." Eddie leaned back and interlaced his fingers over the belly that strained at his shirtfront. "Oh, lordy, that was funny."

"Funny," Henshaw echoed, his eyes elsewhere.

"Easiest money I ever made," Bolan said, playing the part and pulling the bills toward him.

"Franco's a chump. Now, you want a real fight? Digger is your man," Eddie said conspiratorially. He tapped the side of his bulbous nose. "Bastard is as big as a house."

James looked around. "I don't see him."

"Upstairs," Henshaw said. "He's *relaxing*." The emphasis he laid on the word caused Bolan to perk up. He looked at James again, but the other man shook his head in a gesture that Bolan thought meant "I'll tell you later."

Sweets, standing behind the bar, smacked the wood with the butt of his pistol. "Gentlemen, if I could have your attention," he said. The room quieted down. Bolan found that he was grudgingly impressed. Sweets poured himself a drink and knocked it back, then swept the room with a hard gaze. "We all know why we're here."

"Because we're greedy sumbitches," Eddie said loudly. There were a few chuckles.

"There is that," Sweets said. "But it's also because you're the best I got. You've all run tar, tits and Thompsons over the border. Drugs, bodies and guns, and you ain't lost a load, or if you did, don't nobody but you knows it." He poured himself another drink. "But this here run, it'll be a bit different…" Bolan tensed. Sweets smiled. "There'll be more money for one thing."

"And for the other?" James said.

Sweets looked at him. "Fellows we chauffeuring have specific places they want to go. They'll be mixed in with the regulars, and you'll be taking the whole load to different points across the border. They got a schedule, and they're sticklers for punctuality."

"Who are these guys? Tourists?" another man asked.

"Ragheads," Franco spat.

"Customers," Sweets corrected. "Good ones, too, though, ah, probably not repeat ones." He leaned forward over the bar. "There are ten of us and a hundred of them. We'll each be carting ten of them to where they need to go. We'll be meeting them here and shuffling them over."

"A hundred men," James said. "Hell, that's a damn army, Sweets."

"So it is," Sweets said. "And so what? I know a couple of

us done run cartel muscle over the border before, this ain't no different."

"It is if they ain't cartel soldiers," Henshaw barked. His fingers danced nervously along the butt of his pistol. "What was that Franco said? Are we really escorting Jihadists or some mess?"

"What if we are?" Eddie said, looking at the other man. "Their money is as green as anyone else's."

"Yeah, but—"

"Boys, let's be realistic here," Sweets said, interrupting. "What we're talking about is likely treason on some level. Then, so is running undocumented workers or Nicaraguan gunmen into Santa Fe or Dallas. And, if it's tweaking your shriveled little patriotic impulses, need I remind you that every redneck for a hundred miles of the border has a small armory in his basement? It ain't like we're escorting these fellows into the Promised Land. They might blow up a department store or erase a preschool, but at the end of the day, they'll die in the dust same as every other bad man. And we'll be sitting pretty with a nice chunk of cash."

"Yeah, but what about the next time, Sweets?" James said. "We get these guys through and the border is going to close up tighter than blazes."

"Probably, but not for long," Sweets said confidently. "People got short memories. And we provide a necessary function."

Bolan thought that Sweets was kidding himself. There would always be cracks in a border as long and as crooked as the Mexican-American border, but if this scheme succeeded it would mean a death sentence or life imprisonment for every man of Sweets's ilk. Looking around the room, he saw not a few faces that reflected his opinion back at him. None of them, however, were speaking up. Greed could put iron in even the most pliable spine, it seemed.

"Look, I ain't going to force nobody. Give it a minute, talk it over. Have a drink. Let me know," Sweets said, filling up his glass again.

The meeting broke up a moment later. Two or three men stood and wandered outside, lighting up cigarettes as they went and speaking quietly. Bolan stood. "Toilet?" he said. Eddie grinned at him.

"Nervous?"

"Something like that."

"Up them stairs there," Henshaw said, gesturing. Bolan nodded and shot a look at James. The other man inclined his head. Bolan turned toward the stairs, satisfied that the younger man had understood him. He needed to scout the area.

Instincts honed in countless undercover operations prickled in warning as he made his way up the stairs. Like as not, the bulk of the terrorists were waiting for an "all-clear" signal to come into town. But there would have to be someone here to give that signal. And if Bolan were any judge, that man would be the one called Tuerto.

At the top of the stairs, Bolan let his fingers drift toward the pistol clipped to his belt. It wasn't an ideal situation, but he couldn't let pass the opportunity to take the head off the snake first thing, even if he'd have to shoot his way out of town after the fact. His partner wouldn't like it, but Bolan was damned if he was going to let a hundred armed terrorists get anywhere near the American border, sting operation or no sting operation.

The corridor was narrow and there were four doors, two to either side, plus a bathroom that Bolan smelled well before he spotted it. Stepping lightly down the hall, he let his senses drift in such a way as to catch the smallest sound. If you tried to listen for one thing, you almost always missed everything else. But experience had taught him that listening to everything was a sure way not to miss anything.

There was a low buzz of what might have been conversation coming from one room. But from another... Bolan's nostrils wrinkled. He smelled blood and lots of it. He pulled the pistol and went to the latter door, a wordless warning siren pealing in his head as he turned the knob. The door opened on darkness and Bolan stepped through.

It took a moment for his eyes to adjust. The blinds were pulled tight and only a thin drizzle of orange Sonoran light was available to see by. Head cocked, he looked around. There was a bundle wrapped in red-stained sheets on the bed, and the abattoir smell was getting worse for every moment he stood there.

"Who are you?"

Bolan spun quick as a cat, but not quickly enough. A meaty paw slammed down on his wrist and the Executioner found himself jerked into the air and slung back the way he had come before he could do more than blink.

6

The Executioner hit the door at high speed, taking it off its hinges, and bounced off the opposite wall. He rolled to his feet, weaponless, his ears ringing. A monstrous shape filled the doorway. Hands like slabs of cured ham stretched toward him and Bolan narrowly avoided what he knew would surely be a crushing grip. "Who told you that you could come in here?" the man-mountain squalled, sounding more like a petulant child than a monster.

"I was looking for the bathroom, actually," Bolan said, balancing on the balls of his feet. "Guess I made a mistake."

"That was my room! Nobody goes in my room!" A big fist looped out and punched clean through the drywall, showering Bolan with dust. He tried to return the favor, digging his knuckles into a spot just beneath his opponent's sternum. The big man grunted and twisted, pushing Bolan and sending him sprawling down the stairs. "Nobody!"

Bolan clambered to his feet, using the wobbly banister for help. He hadn't been punched that hard in a long time, and he didn't intend to let it happen again. The man was big, a little over Bolan's own six and change in height, and built wide, with a layer of cherubic flab over muscles built by labor, rather than exercise. He was quick, as well, not so much as Bolan, but light on his feet. His eyes bulged and his mouth worked silently as he advanced on the Executioner. Bolan's palm itched for the feel of a pistol. Lacking that, he went for his knife. He ducked under a backhanded swipe and pulled the blade. It closed the gap with his opponent's belly, but viselike fingers swallowed his own, forcing the blade aside. Knuckles scraped his cheek and Bolan brought his knee up. The big man uttered a shrill cry and threw Bolan over the banister as if he weighed no more than a bale of hay.

Bolan hit a table and it broke in two at the point of impact. All the breath had been forced from his lungs and it was all he could do at the moment to roll over and grope for the KA-BAR, which had landed point first into the rough wooden floor. But even as his fingertips found the handle, he heard the ominous click of a gun being cocked. He looked up. The big man glared down at him, a Glock aimed at a point somewhere between Bolan's eyes. Bolan tensed, preparing to roll aside.

A second before his opponent fired, however, there was a second click. The big man stopped dead, his eyes widening as a dark-skinned, one-eyed man pressed the barrel of Bolan's dropped .38 to one pudgy cheek. "I was attempting to sleep," the one-eyed man purred.

"What the hell is going on here?" Sweets cried out, kicking aside the broken chunk of table. He glared first at Bolan, and then up at the tableau above. "Damn it, Digger! What did you do?"

"He came into my room, Django," the big man said, cutting a glance at the man pressing a pistol to his face. "Nobody comes into my room. You said, Django. You said nobody would come into my room."

"I was just looking for the toilet," Bolan said, getting to his feet slowly, the KA-BAR in his hand. Sweets eyed him suspiciously.

"Were you now? Cousin Frank, you do seem to get into fights."

"It's a bad habit," Bolan said, trying for nonchalance. He sheathed the knife. "If it's any consolation, I don't have to go anymore."

Sweets guffawed. Then he looked up at Digger and said, "Mr. Tuerto, if you'd kindly take that gun out of my brother's face, I'd be most obliged."

Bolan fought the urge to whip around. Tuerto! The man with one eye smiled genially and moved down the stairs, the revolver dangling from the trigger guard. He tossed it to Bolan nonchalantly. "I believe that this is yours?" he said.

"Close enough," Bolan said, holstering the weapon. Tuerto smiled again and bowed his head. He looked at Sweets.

"Your men are rowdy," he said.

"Obviously they ain't got enough to do," Sweets said, looking around. The other coyotes had gathered and one or two of them, including James, clutched weapons. The agent met Bolan's eyes and the Executioner gave a slight shake of his head. The younger man relaxed. Sweets looked up at Digger. "Get your room cleaned up, Digger. We're rolling out as soon as the rest of our cargo gets here." Digger turned away without a word. Sweets turned and poked a finger in Bolan's chest. "And you, LaMancha, don't screw with Digger. Otherwise he might just pop your head off. And if he doesn't, I'll shoot you myself."

"Lesson learned," Bolan said.

"Good. Come with me. You, too, James, Eddie," Sweets said. "We got some folks to get loaded." He looked around the bar. "Everybody else, follow as best you can."

"I will come, also," Tuerto said.

"Ain't necessary," Sweets said.

"What is it you Americans say? The customer is always right?"

"I think that's meant in a more general sense, like buying trends and such, but fine," Sweets said. "Whatever floats your boat." Bolan followed the others as they left the cantina, covertly studying Interpol's most wanted as he did so. Tuerto was lean and professional looking, dressed in faded knock-off Levi's and a loose T-shirt. He wore a ragged jacket and could have easily passed for a seasonal worker from south of the border if it weren't for the Seal of Solomon picked out in green thread on the black of his eye patch. His good eye flickered Bolan's way and he drifted toward the Executioner.

"You handled yourself admirably back there," he said.

"I was sloppy," Bolan said, gently prodding the bruise he knew was forming on his jaw.

"Well, yes. But I didn't want to say anything," Tuerto said, grinning. Bolan grunted. "What were you doing up there, if I might inquire?" Tuerto continued.

"Looking for the bathroom," Bolan repeated.

Tuerto looked hard at him. "Were you? I recall that the lavatory was singularly hard to miss."

Bolan glanced at him. His estimation of the man's intelligence, already high, drifted up by several notches. His own eyes narrowed. He decided to go for belligerence. "Are you accusing me of something?"

Tuerto laughed. "Quite the opposite, I assure you." He looked over his shoulder. "You strike me as an intelligent man, Mr....LaMancha, was it?"

"Frank," Bolan said.

"Hello, Frank. Did you smell blood, Frank?"

Bolan blinked. "Yes."

"Ha. Yes. So did I. And being curious, you investigated. What did you see?"

Bolan frowned. Was this professional paranoia or something else? "Nothing much before Magilla used me for a lawn dart."

"Magilla?" Tuerto asked, frowning.

"As in Gorilla…"

Tuerto shook his head. "You saw nothing?"

"Just some bloody sheets."

Tuerto sighed. "Fine, fine, thank you, Mr. LaMancha… Frank."

Bolan processed the disappointment in Tuerto's voice. What had he been hoping for? Was there something here he could use? The Executioner had an instinct for weaknesses; he sought the soft points and found them as often as not. It was what had made him as effective as he was during the years of his long, lonely war. He needed time to confer with James, but would he get it before it was too late?

"Where are we going?" he said out loud, trying to sound curious rather than probing.

"Like I said, to pick up cargo," Sweets said, leading them outside. "If you're hauling contraband, you have got to hide it, Cousin Frank, you know that." He glanced back at Bolan. "Or maybe you don't. Is that why you need money, Cousin Frank?"

"No," Bolan said, remembering James's warning.

Sweets snorted. "You could have fooled me. How about it, Jorge? Cousin Frank bet on the wrong pony?"

"Everybody is hurting these days, Django, you know that." James was trying to act nonchalant, but Bolan could tell how tense he was. He hoped no one else could. He turned slightly and caught Tuerto looking at him, one long finger stroking his eye patch.

Bolan turned away, resisting the urge to touch the .38 resting on his belt.

AMIRA TANZIR SAT in the back of the tractor trailer, its metal walls growing hot beneath the Sonoran sun, and she tried to look as inconspicuous as possible. She had been trained for this, so there was little difficulty. Slump the shoulders, thrust out the feet. Erase all poise and precision and roughen the edges of dignity until it overcame pride. That was how one looked like a peasant, and peasants the world over had a depressing similarity. Dressed in castoff and homespun clothing, she was the very picture of a woman seeking a better life, her natural beauty hidden behind a facade of desperation.

Born in Portugal to a Latin father and an African mother, Tanzir had three degrees and a decade of law enforcement experience. She could speak five languages and four of those fluently, as well as converse in four dialects. She had hunted

Basque separatists through the snowy Pyrenees and faced down detonator-happy would-be martyrs—and had done so with pride. And here she was presently on what was possibly the greatest hunt of her career, in pursuit of one of the most dangerous participants in the War on Terror—El Tuerto.

Eyes closed, she pretended to pray. Instead of catechisms, however, what went through her mind was all that was known about Tuerto. He was the current organizer for the so-called "Holy One Hundred," a splinter faction of al Qaeda whose goals were not so much the establishment of a holy caliphate, as it was to "water Allah's fields with martyr's blood." This likely meant they were planning something big and suitably bloody, rather than the more pedestrian running of a bomb into a military base or shopping mall. No, these men wanted another 9/11; they wanted to leave a burning black scar across America's face. Something Tanzir was determined to prevent at any cost.

But she was even more determined to prevent Tuerto's escape. Unlike his men, he was no martyr. Tuerto was a mercenary, an idealist-for-hire who was far more valuable to his current employers alive than dead for the cause. What little Interpol knew of the operation suggested that he intended to cross the Canadian border within the next few weeks and be on a plane to Algeria soon after. It was his standard M.O.—overseeing operations until just before the net closed and then slipping away.

But just what his current operation was, she didn't know. She blinked, trying to ignore the itch of the contact lenses she wore. They were thicker than what she was accustomed to, and less comfortable than the ones she normally used to change her eye color.

"Stop blinking so much," a quiet voice said in her ear in German. She nearly reached up to touch the flesh-colored communications bud hidden in her ear canal. Instead, she muttered, "How's the picture?"

"Blurry," the voice said. She had to strain to hear it over the rumble of the trailer. She turned her face to the wall of the trailer, ignoring the ovenlike heat radiating from it. No one could hear her, and if they saw her, they'd likely think she was praying, like several others. But there was no sense in taking any chances.

That was what Eugene said, at any rate. Thinking of him made her smile, though only slightly. She was still furious with him, for putting up such a fight with her concerning this assignment. He loved her, she knew, and she loved him, but for all the love between them, he did not truly understand why she had to do this. For all his insight, Eugene Chantecoq did not understand why Tanzir had to be the one to bring Tuerto to heel.

How to explain? she wondered. How to explain the months of grueling work that had gone into so many close calls, so many narrow escapes on Tuerto's part. It was almost futile, the hunting of a man so lucky. But she kept at it, not for anyone else, for any government check or ethereal obligation. No, she hunted Tuerto for herself alone.

It was a selfish thing, she knew. Not good policing. She wasn't being a team player. That was how Control would put it, if he ever bothered to share his opinion with anyone of a lesser rank. "Fuck being a team player," she muttered.

"What?" the voice said, momentarily surprising her.

"Nothing," she grunted. "These contacts are killing me." The lenses were fitted with state-of-the-art transmitters, broadcasting everything she saw back to the joint Interpol-Border Patrol task force at their base of operations. It was cutting-edge technology, which just meant that it was more likely to screw up, in her experience. She fought the urge to blink, and let her hair fall to cover her face.

"Don't mess them up. They're worth more than you."

"I'll remember that," Tanzir muttered. Then, "Has Agent James checked in?"

For a time there was no answer. Then the voice said, "Negative. But our associates assure us that he'll be in position come the time."

Tanzir frowned. She'd only met her partner for this operation briefly, a result of the rushed nature of things. The latter didn't bother her as much as not knowing whether or not she could count on the person who was there to pull her fat out of the fire if things went bad. The American federal agencies had insisted on an American presence in the operation. True to form, Interpol had acquiesced. If this operation had any chance of succeeding, they needed the Americans to do it. Or so Control said.

Personally, she wasn't so sure of that. Besides which, this was her operation, and had been for three years. Three years, she thought, chasing that one-eyed bastard from one country to the next, always arriving just five minutes too late and just in time to pick up the pieces. Unconsciously, her hands clenched and she bit her lip to stifle a grunt of frustration.

"What is your status?" the voice murmured.

She looked around at the packed ranks of humanity huddled in the trailer. All had the same expression…hope, mingled with anxiety and not a little fear. She felt a brief pang of sympathy, which she ruthlessly squashed. "We're being moved to the handoff point now," she said.

"I meant your status. As in you, personally."

Control was, despite the stick up his rear, an observant man. The German knew how she felt, though he'd fully backed her desire to do this. Like as not, he reasoned that her eagerness made her more efficient. It wouldn't do to make him have doubts as to that fact. She didn't intend to let another mission get scrubbed out from under her.

She forced her hands flat. "I'm fine, Control. I'm just fine." Eagerness flooded her. She had hunted as a child, following her father and his friends into the Cadiz Mountains, and the sensation she presently felt was much like she had felt then. The thrill of the hunt was burning in her system.

Tuerto was hers, one way or another.

7

"*Coyotaje* is what you might call an art, Cousin Frank," Sweets said, glancing over his shoulder into the back of the van. "We operate on whatchacall 'social capital,' if you can picture it."

The back of the van was sweltering, and Bolan felt a thin trickle of sweat roll down under his collar. Tuerto, sitting across from him, showed no signs of discomfort. They sat surrounded by heavy crates that smelled of gun oil and packing straw. Bolan hadn't tried for a look inside, but he suspected the contents wouldn't surprise him. Behind them, surfing through the dust kicked up by Sweets's van came three others. If Bolan had been a betting man, he would have put money on each of the other vehicles carrying a similar load of weaponry.

"Are you listening, LaMancha?" Sweets asked. "Best be, because I'm trying to educate you here."

"Oh, give it a rest, Django," Eddie said from the back. The big man had a shotgun resting across his round knees and he rolled his eyes as Sweets laughed.

"Eddie, we can't have no *ignoramuses* running around with us," Sweets said. "Cousin Frank looks sort of dense there, no offense to you, James."

"None taken," James said from the passenger seat. He looked back at Bolan, his face blank. Bolan resisted the urge to smile. The young man was checking on him, making sure he didn't snap and try to throttle the king coyote. If he had known the young agent longer, he might have been insulted.

As it was, Sweets had kept up a steady stream of insults the entire ride. Bolan was honestly beginning to look forward to shooting the man, a rare occurrence for him.

He figured that it was equal parts Sweets testing him and simply being unpleasant. "Social capital, huh?" Bolan spoke up. "I prefer the real thing myself."

"One is transferable to the other, never you fear," Sweets said. "Cartels bring our cargo up from wherever—either South or Central America, it don't matter none—and pay us to take them off their hands and get them the rest of the way into the land of the free and the home of the brave."

"And along the way, they sell the drugs the cartel loaded them down with, and we transfer the money back," Eddie said. "Or we buy guns or some shit and carry that back down to our brothers over the border."

"Guns, in this case." Eddie chuckled, slapping a crate with his palm.

"Cost of doing business. The cartels are giving us ten long-haul trucks full of living, breathing camouflage for Mr. One-Eye's requirements. Least we can do is give them boys some goodies to go home with."

"Broken-down vans and surplus weapons," Eddie said. "The customer gets what the customer wants."

"Rule one of the service industry...they ask, we deliver," Sweets said.

"Professional middlemen," Tuerto said, looking at Bolan. The one-eyed man grinned. "I know a bit about that myself."

"We're a necessary cog in the machine of international commerce is all," Sweets said. "Everybody wants something, and we provide that something, at a price that can't be beat."

"But not for much longer, one would think," Tuerto said, stroking his eye patch. He grinned, baring white teeth. "Not considering the money that I am paying you."

"Speaking of that," Bolan said. "Why not just take a plane? You know, for old times' sake?"

Tuerto looked at him sharply, his one good eye narrowing. The temperature in the back of the van seemed to drop by several degrees. The mercenary's smile held, however. "By land, by sea, by air," he said. He held up three fingers, and bent one. "Planes are *passé,* Frank. This year, it's all about trucks. Next year, boats, I suspect."

"That a fact?" Bolan said, leaning back and crossing his arms.

"You're being impolite, Cousin Frank," Sweets said. "Don't make me come back there and teach you some manners."

Bolan bit back a retort and settled back, looking away. Tuerto continued to look at him for a time, his fingertip tracing the threads that picked out the Seal of Solomon on the patch.

"So, how'd your meeting with Ernesto go, Jorge?" Eddie said with the air of a man trying to change the subject.

"It didn't," James said, after a minute. "He had some trouble in Sinaloa."

"Shame, we could have used a bit of extra cash," Eddie said mournfully.

"Get that thought out of your head right damn now," Sweets said. He glanced at them. "I'm sure our pals from the cartels will have crammed them tractor trailers full of goddamn crank, blow and pigment for a shipment like this."

"I was not informed of this," Tuerto said sharply.

"No? Did I forget to mention it? That was remiss of me, I do apologize," Sweets said. "It's part of doing business with these fellows down here."

"We do not need the additional complications," Tuerto said.

"Rest your pony, Mr. One-Eye," Sweets said, chuckling. "The huddled masses will handle all that. Your boys ain't got to worry about dirtying their martyr-halos with them filthy pharmaceuticals."

"I'm more worried about your men becoming distracted," Tuerto said.

"We might be greedy, but we ain't fools," Eddie said. "Besides, ain't like we got the time to do nothing about it."

"Eddie's right," Sweets said. "We're here."

"Good God, look at all of them," James whispered hoarsely as the tractor trailers came into view, looking like nothing so much as a small fort. Bolan uttered a silent curse as he saw the small sea of waiting people. Half of them were swooning with incipient sunstroke and the other half were looking dehydrated under the glare of the sun.

"Heard tell one time about a less reputable fellow in our line who got squirrely about a drop-off," Eddie said as Sweets put the van in park. "Up and left his whole rig out in the middle of nowhere without ever bothering to open it up. A hundred and fifty of the poor fuckers cooked to death in the back before somebody found it. Said when they opened it up, it looked as if they'd been trying to punch holes in the container with their bare hands to get a little air."

Bolan grimaced as he climbed out and joined the others. Sweets laughed as if Eddie had been telling a funny joke and said, "Are your folks on their way?" He directed the latter to Tuerto. The one-eyed man nodded.

"They should be arriving just as we do. Are you sure these vehicles they're providing can hold loads of these sizes?"

"Heh, I once crammed thirty-four dirt-poor fruit pickers into a station wagon. I think we'll find a way." Sweets smiled and got out.

Bolan eyed the crowd. A quick-and-dirty battlefield estimation let him conclude that there were maybe eighty people waiting on them, possibly more. Bolan's gut churned at the thought of what fate their future held. Hundreds of illegal immigrants, if not more, died every year trying to cross the border between the United States and Mexico.

He leaned against the van and took in the crowd. As he scanned each face, he wondered whether or not that person would make it. He shot a look at Tuerto and Sweets. Would any of those gathered here survive whatever these two had planned? Bolan was realistic enough to know he couldn't save everyone, but he was determined to try regardless.

He came to the decision quickly and with a minimum of re-crimination. To hell with the plans of federal agencies, foreign or domestic; the Executioner, as ever, had his own plans and the will to enact them regardless of the personal consequences.

The hard-faced drivers who had brought the would-be immigrants this far clustered around as Sweets got out of the van. They began speaking rapid-fire Spanish as Sweets held up his arms. "Quiet down, you vultures!" he snarled in English. "I want to check the damn merchandise first."

"I hope he's not being picky for our benefit," Tuerto murmured, looking around coolly. Bolan glanced at the mercenary. Was the man already planning the mass murder of these desperate people...or something further on?

"It's a damn army," Eddie muttered. The heavyset coyote looked at Sweets. "You've really done it this time, you know that? What the hell, man? You think border patrol or the *Federales* ain't noticed a million people just sitting out here in the desert?"

"Calm yourself," Tuerto said. "It has all been planned for. Money was paid, and where bribes would not suffice, blindspots will." He pointed upward. "I suggested this meeting point based on my own research. We are in a natural cross-point between two satellites. By the time anyone sees anything, the image will be hours old and we will be gone."

"Hardly a million of 'em anyway," Sweets drawled, turning away from the drivers. "There's barely a hundred if there's ten."

Eddie shook his head. "This ain't the way we do things, Sweets."

"This is the big time, Eddie," Sweets said without turning around. "We got to take a few risks to make a few bucks."

"This ain't a few risks...this is two really damn big ones," Eddie said. He glanced at Tuerto. "No offense."

"None taken, I assure you," Tuerto said.

"Stop bellyaching," Sweets said, glaring at Eddie. "You agreed to this. No time to back out now." Sweets cocked his head. "Of course, if you insist…" He patted the butt of the pistol riding beneath his arm.

Eddie stepped back a pace, hands up and face pale. "N-no, Sweets! No, I was just saying is all."

Sweets climbed up on top of his van and cupped his hands around his mouth. A moment later he was yelling instructions in broken Spanish at the milling crowd. Bolan drifted toward James. "If we let these people get in those vehicles, they're dead. All of them," he said quietly.

"Think I don't know that?" James replied tonelessly. "I didn't expect this. I mean…I knew it had to be something like this…but not *this*." He shook his head. He looked at Bolan. "What do we do?"

"It'll be messy," Bolan said, hesitating. He looked at the crowd. If he were to enact the plan forming in his head, it was very likely that some of these people would be caught in the crossfire. They would die, and their deaths would be on his head. Bolan was no stranger to such things, but it was not something he could blithely ignore, either. He knew some men who could, and he was thankful he was not one of them. The day human life ceased to have a value for the Executioner was the day his crusade failed.

But in the end, a few probable deaths were as nothing to those certain to occur if the coyotes' deadly cargo reached American soil. Bolan shook his head. "It'll have to be quick. When we get back, I'll get my gear…improvise something."

"The rest of Tuerto's men will have arrived by then," James said doubtfully.

"That's what I'm counting on. Tuerto doesn't trust Sweets—"

"Smart man," James grunted.

"And Sweets likely doesn't trust Tuerto." Bolan looked at the young agent. "I can call my people. What about yours?"

"I can use that phone in my van. We've got a prearranged signal." James looked past Bolan at the crowd of hopeful faces trying to struggle into some semblance of order. "Problem is Tanzir is somewhere in that mess there."

"What? You didn't say anything about that," Bolan said.

"You didn't ask, Cooper," James retorted, fighting to keep his voice low. Bolan backed off, sensing the strain that the young man was under. Sometimes Bolan forgot that life or death wasn't how everyone played the game. At least not on the scale he was used to.

"How were you planning to contact her?" he asked.

"I wasn't. She was supposed to contact me, but how the hell…" He trailed off and shook his head. "I don't see how."

"We may have to move without her. If she's Interpol, she can take care of herself," Bolan said. "We'll—"

There was a shout, and one of the coyotes was sent stumbling by a cartel soldier as he tossed a box of weapons on the ground. The soldier kicked the crate open and shook a weapon at Sweets.

"Whoops," Sweets said. "Looks like my buddy Mendez done found the palomino under the paint."

Bolan looked at the gun in the man's hands and knew instantly what was wrong. The weapon was almost as old as he was, and in bad shape despite the gleam of packing oil. "You're trying to sell them bad guns," he said, looking up at Sweets.

"Good guns cost money," Sweets said nonchalantly. Mendez, the cartel man, shouted again, gesticulating fiercely. Bolan knew he was demanding an explanation, and he tensed. Weapons were being fingered and Bolan felt an electric current in the air; a grim portent of incipient violence. He glanced at James, and saw that the other man felt it, as well.

"Are you going to respond?" Tuerto said tersely.

Sweets said, "Sure," and shot Mendez, his pistol clearing leather in the blink of an eye.

8

Bolan put a round between the eyes of the nearest cartel soldier, sending the man spinning away. The others scattered, hunting for cover. Several of them found it, diving behind a couple of trucks.

"Hell, that's torn it," Eddie said, hefting his shotgun and diving behind the van. James swung behind the van, as well, his own pistol barking. Bolan stood his ground just to Sweets's left, and they fired simultaneously. There had been a dozen cartel drivers; presently there were eight.

Sweets laughed once, a crystal-clear bark that put ripples of disgust the length of Bolan's spine. The coyote had hopped down off the van after shooting Mendez and was stalking through the dust, firing the Parabellum rounds even as he dug under his shirt for a second, smaller pistol holstered at the small of his back. Bolan was tempted to let him get himself shot, but he had already called his own play. He dived for one of the closer vans, the .38 growling to keep the heads of the gunmen down. Bolan's back brushed up against the van and he ripped the door open and threw himself in. Jabbing the parking brake, he set the vehicle to rolling and hurled himself out moments before it crashed into the vehicle the cartel drivers were crouching behind.

There was a shriek of busted glass and bending metal as the vans connected, and men scattered. Bolan found himself out in the open, and he caught one of the fleeing drivers in the head, knocking him down. "Down!" someone yelled. Bolan threw himself flat. Another driver pitched backward, blown off his feet moments before he would have done the same to Bolan.

Bolan glanced back. James saluted him and Bolan shot to his feet. A swirl of dust had risen, whipped up the trucks and the wind. The drivers were all down, eight men dead in as many minutes. Sweets reloaded his pistol as he trotted back toward the others. He grinned at Bolan. "Nice shooting, LaMancha. And that was quick thinking with the truck."

"Seemed like the thing to do," Bolan said.

"Looks like most of our cargo hightailed it, Sweets," Eddie said, red-faced and breathing heavy. "We got maybe fifty, sixty folks left."

"Good enough," Sweets said, holstering his pistol. "Less for Tuerto's boys to get rid of later."

"Get rid of?" the coyote said. Tuerto shrugged and Eddie paled. "Man…" he muttered.

"Don't get a conscience on me now, Eddie," Sweets chided. "Let's get these doggies loaded up. Rawhide!" He chuckled and walked toward the would-be migrants, hands raised.

Bolan looked around, slightly surprised that there was still anyone left. James stood beside him. "Where else are they gonna go, man?" he said. "Most of 'em paid with everything they owned to get this far. A little gunplay ain't going to scare them off now."

"No," Bolan said, trying to ignore the sick feeling growing down deep in his gut.

"Good news is that I spotted Tanzir," the agent continued.

"Where is she?" Bolan said.

"Right where she's supposed to be," James said.

As far as unexpected events went, the brief gun battle had been number eight on Tanzir's list. She joined the group crowding around the van and tried to calm the jitters that sprang up the moment she caught sight of a familiar profile. She had only been this close to him once before, just after an explosion in a morning market in some no-name little town in North Africa. He had sipped coffee as body parts rained down and then had calmly paid his bill and wandered away into the confusion. Tuerto. Mr. One-Eye.

She couldn't say for certain how he'd escaped that day, or whether or not he'd seen her when he turned and looked in her direction moments before the bomb went off. Control had assured her that her cover had not been blown then, or on this day.

With his looks and dusky coloration, she judged him to be a Berber rather than an Arab. A neatly clipped beard and shaved head gave him the look of a particularly well-fed bird of prey, and his eyes were cold rather than burning with fanaticism. That coldness was what made him more dangerous than the lunatics who followed him, she knew.

Rittermark and the others—even Chantecoq—didn't see it. They didn't understand Tuerto the way that she did; they thought that he was just one more terrorist on the United Nations' list. But she knew better. Tuerto wasn't a monster, he was a monster-maker. He put together the plans, bought the explosives, armed the martyrs. He set up the dominoes for maximum coverage, and then skipped clear, wealthy on blood money.

He cared nothing for God or country; he held to no ideology save that of Mammon. And he would not hesitate to vanish if he felt the noose closing around his neck.

She had been more relieved than she'd thought she would be when she caught sight of Agent James during the brief gun battle. She smiled slightly, thinking of the look on his face. He was, by all rights, an effective undercover agent. Or so she had been told. But he had looked like a deer in headlights to her when the shooting began. She pushed the thought aside. This was not the time. She had more important matters to attend to.

Thinking back on it, this was probably the part of the mission that Chantecoq had been less than pleased with. She smiled. She wasn't exactly happy about it herself.

Drawing close to Tuerto, she mustered her courage, and stumbled into him. Strong fingers gripped her shoulders and jerked her upright. The one good eye met hers and she essayed a smile. "I apologize, sir," she said in Spanish.

"Think nothing of it. I have been hit by less pleasant things, I assure you," he replied in the same language. He released her almost as an afterthought, and she reached out to steady herself. He blinked. "You are traveling to the States?"

"God willing," she said, crossing herself.

"Ma'sa'Allah," he said. "Are you alone then? In my country, a woman such as you would not travel by herself."

She stepped closer to him to allow others to move past her and back into the truck. "I have no one else," she said. "And I have nowhere else to go."

"That is…unfortunate," he said. He brushed a strand of hair out of her face. "And you would even face bullets to go somewhere else?" he continued, jerking his chin toward the bodies contorted in the dust.

"I would," she said, not looking at them. Death did not bother her as much as it had when she'd first started, but even so, she preferred not to see the human detritus of such confrontations.

"Ha," he said, smiling slightly.

"We ain't got time for this," the leader of the smugglers— Sweets—growled. He seized Tanzir's wrist in a painful grip and jerked her aside and shoved her into the truck. "In you go, sweetheart!" She landed on someone's lap and struggled to her feet even as the door slammed shut with a loud clunk. In the sweltering darkness, Tanzir smiled.

He was hers.

"Rude," Tuerto murmured, fixing Sweets with a look. Sweets shrugged in his infuriating way.

"We ain't got time for you to paw the filly right here, right now. That little tussle just now put us behind schedule. Whatever you want to do with her after we get going is your business."

Tuerto felt slightly insulted. "I am no beast. I am on a holy mission." He frowned. "And that 'tussle,' as you call it, was your fault."

Sweets looked at him insolently. "Yeah, sure, whatever, let's go."

They climbed aboard the van and Sweets put it in gear. They bounced back toward town, the trucks following. Tuerto sat back and thought of the girl. She was not a peasant, no matter how she dressed. But, of course, it was not unheard of for political refugees to mingle with those seeking work. It would explain the soft burr to her accent, not quite like the liquid sound of the locals. From farther south perhaps? Guatemala? Argentina? Bolivia? He smiled. She was beautiful. And brave...two qualities that Tuerto found irresistible.

And something else...she was familiar. He did not know how, or why, but she was familiar to him. It didn't matter, he supposed.

Still, perhaps this trip wouldn't be all business after all. The cross-country trek to Canada would be more pleasant with female companionship, that was for certain. Of course, he would have to ask her name first. He leaned his head back and closed his eye, thinking pleasant thoughts.

He opened it again, a moment later, as a thought occurred to him. "Will the cartels come looking for their guns?"

"Probably. But not any time soon. Few days, maybe a week, they'll begin to wonder, and in wondering, they'll get suspicious and then they'll troop out here and find...what? Some burned-out vans and some skeletons. Who knows what happened? Maybe them boys they sent done plumb run off with them guns, you know?"

"It's a risk," Tuerto said.

Sweets shrugged. "So was shooting ol' Mendez. Got to

take a risk to make a buck, that's what my daddy always said, God bless him."

"LaMancha reacted quickly. Far quicker, in fact, than anyone else," Tuerto said.

"Oh, he's a special one, him," Sweets said. "I got my eye on him."

"Is there something I should know?" Tuerto said.

"Nope," Sweets said. "Just a leak in the tank is all."

Tuerto grunted. "You think he's a spy?" he said.

"Oh, I know he is," Sweets said. His grin turned feral. "See, I got me a phone call earlier today about ol' Jorge, intimating as he was not entirely on the up-and-up. A whiff of deception, as you might put it."

"Ah," Tuerto said. "But no proof?"

"Proof is in the pudding. I might have let it slide, but Cousin Frank done stirred it up. Too slick that boy. Too good."

"Yes," Tuerto murmured. "Though I dare say that your brother handled him easily enough."

"Digger's like a rhino. Not much can stop him once he charges," Sweets said with no small amount of pride. "Still, Jorge and his bogus cousin will get theirs, never you fear, Mr. One-Eye." Sweets's grin threatened to split his face. "Never you fear."

9

"So, what's the plan?" James said as they drove.

Bolan looked up and smiled stonily. "Reading my mind?"

"No, reading your face. You've got that look a guy gets right before he goes off-book," James said.

"How were you planning on tracking all these vehicles? To catch them all, I mean?" Bolan said.

"Once I ID'd all the faces involved, I was going to get in touch with the bosses. Everyone involved in this has got a record, and they've all got their sweet spots for doing a border run. Border patrol, the Feebs, whoever else will be waiting," James said.

"Sloppy," Bolan said flatly. "What happens if they go a different route?"

"They won't," he said confidently and tapped his head. "It ain't in them to break habit. Habit is what keeps guys like Sweets and Eddie out of prison on a long-term basis. There'll be copters in the air, as well. I've got a GPS tracker on my ride, so they'll be following me. No, the big problem is catching Tuerto. He's the big fish. Interpol wants him, the FBI wants him…heck, the CIA wants him. And I bet your bosses do, as well, if they know about it by now." James looked at him. "Our way, we catch them by surprise, before they get to their targets, whatever those might be. So, what's your way?"

"Like I said, my way, they don't get out of this town, especially Tuerto. And they don't get the chance to finish their mission." He took a breath. "How far from the border are we?"

"Far enough that we're out of U.S. jurisdiction," James said. "That's why we want them to come over the border, after all."

"And what would it take to get the *Federales* involved, you think?" Bolan said.

"They're already involved. Though if I know my bosses, they haven't bothered to alert our southern cousins as to the exact date and time," James said, smiling sourly.

Something in the young man's voice caught Bolan's attention. "But?"

"But I might have, ah, let something slip to a few local law enforcement professionals of my acquaintance in these parts." James ducked his head. "Seemed only polite."

"That might not have been the wisest course of action," Bolan said. "If Sweets has contacts inside their organization, as well…"

"Then we're screwed. Nothing to do now but play the cards we're dealt," Jorge said. "You don't win the game unless you bet, Cooper."

Bolan liked the young man's bravado. "Fair enough. So, here's my thinking…if we made enough noise, do you think anyone would come running?"

"Lots of folks." James frowned. "But won't that just make it harder to predict where anyone is going?"

"Not if no one gets out of the town," Bolan said, his voice going grim. "Oh, make no mistake, if the federal government was dealing with cartel soldiers or run-of-the-mill criminals, I'd have no problems with the plan your bosses concocted. But terrorists aren't criminals, at least not in the way we're used to thinking of them. They're foreign combatants, and these will be on enemy soil. They won't be looking to do anything but cause as much damage as possible to as many targets as possible. And trying to round them all up your way will only give them a wealth of targets to aim at. They'll fight to the death. Any death."

The border patrol agent nodded jerkily. "Sweets wants to leave at dark-thirty or thereabouts. And not everyone will be leaving at once. Too conspicuous, even for the guys Sweets has bribed. So we've got until then. How do we do this?"

"Simple. We make sure that you're the first to leave," Bolan said. "And that you've got Tuerto and Tanzir on board."

"Doesn't sound so simple," James said dubiously.

"It will be." Bolan patted the knife on his hip. "Now, drop me off just outside of town."

"Outside of—?" James looked at him. "What are you planning to do?"

"Making sure things stay simple," the Executioner said simply.

James dropped him off without further comment, and Bolan crept back into town as the sky was going orange. It seemed even more crowded than before, and Bolan knew at once that Tuerto's men had arrived, as well. They lounged in doorways and on porches, watching the vehicles stop and the engines go quiet. Bolan avoided the main thoroughfare and climbed a broken bluff overlooking the town. From what he could glean from the setup, it had likely been a mining town once, before the desert had crept up over it and driven its inhabitants in one direction or another.

Low-crawling through the scrub brush and dirt on the slope of the bluff, Bolan paused to collect himself. Sweets was overconfident, and hadn't left any sort of guards on the vehicles that the coyotes would be using to transport their deadly cargo. But Tuerto was another matter. Hunkering low, Bolan saw two men sitting near the vehicles, smoking and speaking quietly. One carried an AK-47, the other merely a pistol. Neither one was looking in his direction.

He considered his options. Quiet or loud? Both had their

perks, but he knew the latter was more trouble than it was worth in this situation. Quiet it was.

Thus decided, Bolan snatched up a rock and gave it an overhand toss. It bounced and clattered down the screed. Both men looked up at once. The one with the AK started forward after a moment, his eyes narrowing as he tried to pierce the dim shadows of the gloaming. Bolan pressed himself flat and waited, barely breathing. Then, just as the man moved past him, he rose up and fastened a big hand around the man's mouth and nose and drove the tip of the KA-BAR up through his back, angling the blade to pierce the lungs and remove any chance the man had to warn his companion. Carrying the body to the ground, Bolan dragged it aside and out of immediate sight. Then, as patient as any predator, he waited.

He didn't have to wait long. The second man clambered up the screed, calling out softly to his companion. "Farouk?" he said, one hand on the butt of the pistol holstered beneath his arm. "Farouk?"

Bolan took a guess from the man's accent and grunted, in Farsi, "Up here." The guess looked to have been the correct one, as the man came closer. Bolan sent another rock tumbling. The man spun and Bolan sent him to the same fate that had claimed Farouk. Wiping the blade clean on the dead man's shirt, he sheathed it and moved carefully toward the vehicles. They had all been parked close together beneath a stretched awning of leather and camouflage netting that James had said was a coyote trick to avoid detection in this era of flybys and eyes in the sky. Drug runners did much the same when hiding their boats or trucks. It was a new age, and Bolan every so often felt wrong-footed by it.

Luckily this time it just made his job easier. Staying low, he approached the first truck. Checking it, he climbed up and lifted the hood. Moving briskly, he removed the spark plugs, tossing them out into the desert. He moved to the next and did the same. On the third, he swept his knife out and punctured the brake lines one by one. On the fifth and sixth, he rolled beneath them and cut the fuel lines with efficient slashes. On seven, eight and nine, he ruined the radiators, letting the antifreeze and water drain out onto the greedy ground. With ten, he simply cut the ignition wires.

He avoided James's van, which left only four viable vehicles in the town—two small trucks and two vans. His plan was simple enough; smaller vehicles meant smaller groups. And if what James had told him about Tuerto was on the money, the man with one eye would damn well make sure he was on the first bus out when the shooting started. And the enigmatic Tanzir would be right with him, Bolan was certain.

He smiled thinly. When James had pointed her out, Bolan had watched as she threw herself at Tuerto. It was an interesting gambit, if a bit old-fashioned. But it made sure that she would have a reason to be around when he left. He knew it must churn the agent's stomach, however, to play nice with the man she'd been hunting for three years. Bolan had seen the flash of raw loathing in her eyes as she leaned against him, and was surprised that her target hadn't. Maybe having only one eye made it harder to look past a pretty face. Bolan's smile turned grim.

He went to James's van and opened the hidden compartment and grabbed his gear, sliding the body armor on and then the web gear. He slung his H&K over his shoulder and hefted the satellite phone. One call to Brognola, and he would be done.

"Time to call in the cavalry," he muttered, retreating up the hill.

THE WOMAN HAD WINGS beneath her skin, Digger knew. He watched her as she climbed out of the back of the truck with the rest, her hair as black as oil and her skin like cinnamon. She was all smooth muscle and grace and his palms itched to see the black bird nestled in her breast. He gave a grunt and pushed away from the clapboard wall, his nostrils flaring. Sweets was trotting toward the cantina, beating dust off his clothes. Digger grabbed his arm. "I want that one in my load," he said, gesturing to the ragged group of migrants being herded into a building.

Sweets looked at him, then back at the girl. "This ain't the time for you to be indulging, baby brother. We got more important things to worry about."

"I want her," Digger whined.

Sweets tore his arm loose from his brother's grip. "You always want them!" he hissed. "And don't I give them to you? Don't I take care of you? Like that girl today, huh?"

"Yes, but—" Digger cut his eyes away. Sweets grabbed his chin and forced the big man to look at him.

"No buts! Now ain't the time!" Sweets snarled. "And clean up that damn room. The ragheads can smell your leavings."

Digger's face flushed and he pulled away, head bowed. He looked like a scolded child. Sweets knew that in some ways that was exactly the case. In other ways his brother was as far from a child as it was possible to get and still be human. He had taken care of Digger since their mother's unfortunate passing, the less said of which, the better, as far as Sweets was concerned. He loved his brother, but on occasion he wished that he had shot and dumped him in a ditch somewhere on that nasty day he'd found him crouched over their momma.

But he hadn't, and he didn't really know why. Sweets was a hollow man, full of cold and dark, but his brother was something else entirely. Digger was fit to bursting with something raw and bright and sometimes, when he got agitated, Sweets thought he could catch a glimpse of it. He sighed and patted Digger's cheek. "I'm sorry, Digger. Do what you need to do… I'll see that she's in there. But you wait, hear me? You wait until you dump them ragheads. I'm counting on you. Business before pleasure."

Digger's face twisted up into a smile. "You can count on me, Django. I'll see to it. I'll do it good."

"Yeah, I know you will," Sweets said, clapping him on the back and leaving his brother to stare longingly at the object of his desire.

"EVERYONE IS HERE THEN?" Tuerto said, checking the clip of his pistol with exceeding care. "Everyone knows their part?"

"The Holy One Hundred have assembled," Abbas said with the air of one intoning Holy Scripture. "We will drive the lance of Islam into the belly of Satan!" The other eight men in the room above the cantina murmured agreement. Along with Abbas and Tuerto, they made for the ten heads of the Holy One Hundred; nine men, handpicked by Tuerto for their expertise in motivating large groups and their unyielding fanaticism.

"Ma'sa'Allah," their leader said, holstering his pistol. "Do not count the dragon slain before you have gotten the lance in position, my friends."

"Is that not what we are doing now? Getting our lance into position? What can stop us?" Abbas said.

"A depressingly large number of things, I'm afraid. That is why I had Farouk and Hassid watch the vehicles," Tuerto said. "We are not in America yet, gentlemen. There are still any number of hurdles we must cross, not including the border. When you reach your destination, terminate your transportation."

"And the others? The Mexicans?"

Tuerto hesitated. "Leave them. They will scatter. The authorities will not be able to track them."

"But—"

"Leave them, I said. They are neither a threat nor a target in our war upon America. This has to do with them not being Americans, you see," he said bitingly. "We will shed no blood save that which is necessary."

"Is this because of the woman, Berber?" Abbas said, his eyes narrowing. "Is that whore's welfare such a concern, and you having only just met her?" He snorted. "I saw the way you eyed that one as you returned."

Tuerto paused, and turned a slow, steady eye upon the other man. Abbas blanched and stepped back. But, seeing his comrades around him, he regained some of his backbone. "Well? Explain yourself? I saw you fawning over her…it is disgraceful to see a holy warrior act so!"

Tuerto laughed. "Holy warriors? Is that what we are? I was under the impression that you were terrorists and I was a mercenary," he said disdainfully. "I make no judgments on your cause, Arab, but do not call it something that it is not. And do not presume to lecture me on morality."

Abbas flushed and his hand went for his gun. Tuerto was quicker. The barrel of his pistol pressed the end of Abbas's nose flat. "Your leaders have given me leave to do as I see fit to carry out their work. That means I can use and abuse my tools as I see fit, as long as it serves their purpose. You are a tool, Abbas. A blunt object I will employ to facilitate al Qaeda's operations efficiently. If you have any objections in that regard, please feel free to take them up with Allah, in his infinite mercy, when you see him." Tuerto smiled and cocked the pistol. "Of course, an appointment can be arranged immediately, if you cannot wait."

Abbas's mouth sagged open and he flailed backward. The others stepped aside and he fell to the floor in fear, his eyes locked on the barrel of the gun. For a moment, Tuerto felt a brush of sympathy for the man. Abbas was not a coward—no man who intended to martyr himself could be—but there was a difference between dying for a purpose and being shot out of hand for talking too much. Allah, perhaps, in his wisdom, did not deliver a bounty of virgins upon those who entered paradise via the latter route.

"'Oh, my warriors, where would you flee? Behind you, the desert. Before you, the enemy. You have left now only the hope of your courage and your constancy. Remember that in this country you are more unfortunate than the orphan seated at the table of the avaricious master. Your enemy is before you, protected by an innumerable army. He has men in abundance, but you, as your only aid, have your own swords, and, as your only chance for life, such chance as you can snatch from the hands of your enemy,'" Tariq recited as he lowered his pistol. He looked around the room. "That was said the first time my people—our people—invaded the lands of the infidel. Hopefully, we will be just as successful as that ancient conqueror."

JAMES TRIED HIS BEST not to look nervous as Sweets gathered the drivers together. No one had noticed that they were one man short yet, and James intended that they never did. The head coyote stood on the cantina steps, sipping a beer. "Alrighty, boys, we got us twenty until we start to haul ass, so here's how we're breaking this down. When it's time to go, you go and grab some local color and head to your vehicle. Mr. One-Eye here will see to the dispensation of his people, as it were, and your passengers will be waiting. After that, you got your route and your usual dump points, so you just do what you do best and we'll all be kicking back on the beach with more money than God."

"Who drives out of here first?" someone said.

"I'll do it," James said.

Sweets looked at him. "Eager to get out of here, Jorge?"

"Eager to count that money, Django," James said.

"Ha. I bet you are. But no, Digger is going first." Sweets nodded to the big man, who was slumped against the wall, hands in his pockets.

"Why him?" Eddie said.

"Because I say so, Eddie. And after Digger, it'll be Franco. Then Henshaw and Morris, and you, Eddie. Then Purfoy, Creasey, Jorge and Maxie. And last, but not least, *myownself*." Sweets tapped his chest for emphasis. "That's fair, right?" he said, looking at James.

"I suppose," he said, shrugging. "When do we get our money?"

"Half up front and half when you make your drop-off," Sweets said, crumpling his beer can and tossing it aside. "I already put the envelopes under your seats. Quick enough for you?"

"It'll do." James's mind whirled. He needed to keep them talking and keep them distracted. "What'll we do with the regulars when Tuerto's men get off? Or are we just dropping the whole load?"

"The ragheads will handle it," Franco said, snickering. "Right, Sweets?"

"Right as the rain in Spain, Franco." Sweets swept the gathering with his eyes. "Make no mistake, boys...this'll be the easiest money you ever made, so long as you don't screw it up. Speaking of which, where did Cousin Frank go, Jorge? Looking for the bathroom again?"

"I ain't his keeper," James said.

"Oh, but you are," Sweets said. He scratched his nose and hopped off the steps. "You are indeed his keeper, Jorge, just like I'm Digger's keeper. Family watches out for family. Unless they ain't really family. Is that the case here, Jorge?"

James hesitated. "What are you trying to say?"

"I'm saying a little bird told me, in the most delightful accent, that you might be playing a game on us, your fellow brothers in brigandry." Sweets's smile spread like fire across oil. "I got a call from a friend of mine in the *Federales,* Jorge."

James's blood turned to ice. Bolan had been right. "Look, Sweets, I can explain..."

"Explain what? That you turned us all over to the Mexican cops? Lucky for us, they're slow as molasses and we'll be gone before they show up. But you...I figure you'll be here waiting for them. You might not be in any condition to talk, though. Somebody grab him, please."

James swept his pistol out and swung it around, forcing the

other men to back off. "You got this all wrong, Sweets!" he said, trying to salvage something.

"I had hoped so, but then I saw you come into town with Cousin Frank. I told you not to bring nobody, Jorge. That was mistake one. Mistake two, if you're interested, was letting your pal Frank go snooping around. In this business, Jorge, old buddy, you don't get no mistake three." Sweets pulled his pistol. "Drop the gun and it'll be quick."

"Sweets, you need me!" James said, shouting. Maybe if Cooper heard him, he'd know to go to ground and stay out of sight. He had no doubt that the man from the Justice Department could take care of himself, but even he couldn't fight this many men by his lonesome.

"We'll make do, I expect. The world abides, Jorge. Never think it doesn't," Sweets said.

James shook his head. "I guess now's as good a time as any to tell you that I don't know what in the hell you're talking about half the time, Sweets."

"I'm a philosopher, what can I say? Drop the piece, Jorge."

"Nope," James said, looking around at the men surrounding him. In the wild, coyotes often turned on the sick or injured. So it was with the men who had taken this animal's name as a badge of honor.

"I guess we do it the hard way, then," Sweets said, grinning. A second later, he pulled the trigger.

10

Bolan glanced back at the town just as the setting sun caught on something metal. "Hold on a minute," he said, pulling the phone away from his ear. His eyes narrowed. Was that a gun? His fingers flew to his harness and he unclipped the small binoculars neatly folded up there. The town sprang into focus and he saw Agent James surrounded by hostiles. Bolan cursed.

"Striker?" Hal Brognola said, his voice echoing out of the phone. "Striker, respond!"

Bolan jerked the phone up as he began to make his way down the slope. "I'm here. You've got the coordinates?"

"Yes, but I don't know if I'm going to be able to pull enough strings to organize something like this. Wouldn't you rather have a team from the Farm?" Brognola said almost pleadingly. Bolan would have laughed, if he'd had the time. While politics was Brognola's bread and butter, sometimes the byzantine bureaucracies of Washington were almost too much for even the ex-FBI man to bear. Add in Interpol and the Mexican government and you had one hell of a jurisdictional mess, even before Bolan had stuck his nose in, and it was just going to get worse.

"Do what you can," Bolan said.

"What about you?"

"I'll be doing what I can," Bolan said. "Striker out." He turned the phone off, stuffed it out of sight and hefted his H&K. Sliding past the vehicles, he edged into town. He could hear James's voice loud and clear, and knew that the man was attempting to warn him off. A burst of admiration filled him. It wasn't every day that he encountered someone who was willing to throw his own life away to warn a man he'd just met. He would have to find some way of repaying that debt.

Sighting several lounging terrorists, Bolan crept toward them, around the back of the building. They were armed, but watching the confrontation intently, though more like spectators than sentries. Bolan grinned mirthlessly. Raising the H&K, he sighted on one of the coyotes, the one standing closest to Franco. Creasey, he thought. Then, with a yell, Bolan cut loose. The coyote did a whirling dance and then toppled to the ground. Franco spun, his eyes going wide. Bolan ducked down even as Tuerto's men stood and looked around.

"Goddamn ragheads!" Franco snarled, firing his pistol. "It's a setup!"

Yes, but not the kind you think, Bolan thought. Franco shot the closest of Tuerto's men, his pistol sowing a crop of red flowers across the man's torso. The terrorist's companions raised their weapons with alacrity and returned fire, stitching Franco with enough lead to open a pencil factory. The coyote fell back, and his body hit the dirt, and the town exploded in gunfire.

Bolan ripped a smoke canister off his harness, popped the pin with his thumb and tossed it out into the chaos. Then he did it again, tossing another canister in the opposite direction. Soon the street was filled with colored smoke as bodies stumbled through it, coughing. Bolan dived into the smoke, a handkerchief wrapped around his mouth and nose. He had to find James and quick.

A form stumbled toward him, pistol swinging around. Bolan didn't recognize the outline and he stepped aside, bringing the butt of his H&K down on the back of the man's skull, dropping him flat. Bullets punctured trails of air through the smoke as he headed for the last place he'd seen James. The last he'd seen of him, he'd been nose to pistol with Sweets, which wasn't a healthy place to be, in Bolan's opinion.

Behind him, he heard the scrape of boot heels on sand. "Hiya, Cousin Frank," Sweets said, coughing. Bolan, always light on his feet, threw himself aside as the Parabellum spat angry hornets into the dirt. Bolan rose to his feet and drove the length of the H&K into Sweets's belly, causing him to double over. Bringing the weapon up rapidly, he caught the coyote beneath the chin, knocking him onto his ass. Sweets groaned and tried to crawl to his feet and Bolan gave a moment's thought to letting him. Then, common sense made him bring his gun around.

Before he could fire, however, a shadow fell over him. Two seconds later, it was followed by two heavy hands, which wrapped themselves in his combat harness and jerked him from his feet. He was lifted into the air and thrown like a round of shot out of a cannon. Rolling through the dust and smoke, Bolan dug his fingers into the hard, sunbaked clay of the street and righted himself. Digger charged toward him like a bull-elephant, hands reaching, teeth bared. The big man didn't look as if he'd be stopped by anything short of death.

Bolan fired, but not quickly enough. A wide hand swatted the barrel aside even as it spoke and a fist like a sledgehammer caught him a glancing blow on the side of the head. Dizzy, the Executioner twisted, reaching for thick wrists and planting his foot on one large instep. Despite the ringing in his ears, he managed to toss Digger over his hip. As the coyote ate dust, his brother was already jogging toward Bolan, pistol extended.

James crashed out of the smoke and into Sweets, his fist cracking across the other man's jaw. Sweets fell and James stumbled past, into Bolan's arms. "Think our cover is blown, Cooper." He coughed weakly. There was a red patch on his shirt, and Bolan felt a chill course through him. Unfortunately, there was no time to check on his well-being.

"You might be right," Bolan said, swinging around to put himself between James and the three men who stepped out of the dispersing smoke, automatic rifles raised. The Executioner beat them to the punch, firing as he shoved the border patrol agent into a run. "Go! Go!" James began to run awkwardly and, without stopping to see whether he'd taken down his targets, Bolan followed.

"Sorry about this, Cooper." James coughed. "Guess…guess you were right, huh?"

"It happens," Bolan said. "We need to get to one of those trucks and get out of here, fast. This way… Damn it!" He heard shouting and men rushed out from between the buildings ahead, weapons clutched tight. They hesitated, not recognizing the situation for what it was. Bolan didn't give them the chance. He opened up on the tightly clustered group, cutting them down like chaff. James's pistol echoed his gun by mere seconds, Bolan was pleased to note. There was fight left in the young man yet. He dragged James past the bodies and into a space between buildings. The man's head was lolling and the stain on his shirt was larger than Bolan remembered.

Setting James down as gently as possible, Bolan ripped open his shirt and examined the wound, determining swiftly that the bullet was lodged in the meat of his chest. A brief pressure test revealed that the other man's collarbone was likely cracked, as well, if not broken. He ejected the spent clip and reloaded the H&K before he knelt beside the wounded man.

Pulling his KA-BAR out, he dug the tip into the wound and enlarged it slightly, just enough for him to dig a finger in and dislodge the bullet. Then, pulling a sterile field dressing out of his harness, he slapped it on the wound and made a bandage out of James's shirt, binding him up and immobilizing his arms and shoulders. With a grunt, Bolan scooped him up into a modified fireman's carry. James groaned.

"You'd rather I leave you?" Bolan said, hurrying forward.

"Can't a man groan without somebody making a case out of it?" James whimpered.

A moment later, they sighted the vehicles. Bolan heaved James into the passenger seat of the man's van and climbed up into the driver's seat a moment later. A bullet plucked at the door frame even as he opened it, and he turned, the H&K giving a burp as he stroked the trigger.

"Stop them!" someone yelled.

Bolan threw himself into the cab and started the engine. "Hold on!" he roared, slapping the gear to R and stomping on the gas. The van shot backward and there was a short sharp scream as something squelched beneath the big all-terrain wheels. Growling in satisfaction, Bolan jerked the gear to D and the van rumbled forward. But not for long.

A wood-paneled truck lunged forward and T-boned Bolan. Both vehicles spun, locked together in a mess of mangled metal. Broken glass peppered Bolan's face and hands and he clawed for the Desert Eagle on his hip as his vehicle slammed sideways against a building that gave out a titanic groan of bruised timbers. Bolan rolled around and kicked out the broken windshield. Ignoring the bone-deep ache in his limbs and joints, he clambered out. Smoke and steam jetted out from beneath the crumpled hoods of both vehicles. Bolan, dizzy from the impact, took unsteady aim at the other truck's windshield and fired twice, shattering it.

His mind tried to catch up to his body, and he turned to see to James, but a number of bodies climbed up onto the trucks and tackled him. Big and strong as he was, Bolan was in no shape to take on multiple opponents. He was thrown to the ground and found himself face-to-face with several very familiar pairs of feet. Spitting dirt and blood, Bolan looked up at Django Sweets.

"Cousin Frank, damned if you didn't disappoint me," Sweets said. Then he drove the toe of his boot into Bolan's temple, further scattering his thoughts into a disjointed cloud. The last thing he heard before blackness hit him was Sweets saying, "Get his ass up."

THE SIZZLE OF BURNING MEAT awoke Bolan from his daze. A moment later, the pain hit and with a grunt he began to buck in his seat, his muscles spasming unconsciously. The knife was pulled back from his neck, its white-hot blade hissing softly as it whipped through the cool air of the Sonoran night, trailing greasy smoke. Bolan shook the sweat from his face and looked around. He was in a chair, held in place by a tow chain that had been wrapped around him and padlocked. The skin where his neck and shoulder met ached and he grimaced as he felt blood trickle down his bare chest.

"What do you see?" Digger said softly, stabbing Bolan's KA-BAR back into the coals that glowed redly in the small portable grill. Bolan's chair was in front of the big man's bed, and Digger had a host of unpleasant-looking implements scattered across its surface. He thrust Bolan's knife deeper into the coals and shifted it with his fingertips. "Do you see it?" the big man said, looking at him in an almost plaintive manner.

"I see something," Bolan said harshly.

"What?"

"A dead man."

Digger blinked and then nodded. "Okay," he said, pulling the knife out of the coals and pressing it lightly against the skin of Bolan's stomach. Smoke hissed upward and Bolan tightened his muscles, resisting the urge to scream as his flesh cooked and curled. "What about now?" Digger said gently.

The windows were open, and Bolan could hear men arguing and metal crashing. He focused on the sounds as he tried to block out the pain. He had been tortured more than once in his long war, but it wasn't something you could truly prepare yourself for. All you could do was suck it up and take it. Eyes closed, he concentrated on his breathing as the flat of the knife slid up and around across his belly. Boots scraped on wood and Bolan's eyes opened as a thin shape pushed away from the wall.

"Stop it, Digger. I want to talk to him," Sweets said.

Digger didn't stop. "You said I could," he said.

"And I'm saying stop, baby brother."

"But—" Digger tossed the knife aside and lumbered to his

feet, face twisting. Sweets met the mad glare with an empty stare and the two men looked at each other for long moments before Digger let out a breath and looked away. "I hate you," he said petulantly.

"No, you don't," Sweets said, patting him on the arm. "Go get a drink. I'll let you get back to it in a bit. Go on." He chivied his brother out of the room and closed the door behind him. He looked at Bolan. "No worries, Cousin Frank. I'll make this quick as critters."

"Don't…don't hurry on my account," Bolan wheezed, fighting to keep his head up. He felt like an overcooked sausage. His skin was flushed and his arms and shoulders were hurting.

Sweets laughed. "Still got a sense of humor? That's good. Look on the bright side, that's what I say."

"There's a bright side?" Bolan said, surreptitiously testing the chains that held him. Sweets sat on the bed in front of him.

"Well, you'll be dead soon. That's got to count for something," Sweets said, grabbing a handful of Bolan's hair and yanking his head back. "Pay attention. I got some questions."

"As do I," Tuerto said, pushing the door open and startling Sweets. Behind the one-eyed man was another of his men, the big man named Fahd. "Perhaps our questions are the same, eh?"

"Maybe, but I'm asking mine right now, so why don't you get lost," Sweets said, rising to his feet.

"I think not. In fact, I am contemplating cutting you out of the equation entirely, my friend," Tuerto said. Sweets flushed.

"Yeah? That so?"

"What would you do in my place?" Tuerto shrugged eloquently, hands spread. "It is obvious that your operation is not so watertight as you assured me. What other assurances, then, should I question?"

"Maybe you should look at your own guys," Sweets said. "Interpol don't concern itself with illegals, last I looked."

It was Tuerto's turn to flush. A muscle in his jaw jumped and Sweets laughed.

"Quiet," Tuerto said.

Sweets chuckled. "Nah, I like to talk." He raised his hands. "Know what, though? I got me some work to do thanks to Cousin Frank here, so you have at it," he said. "But…" He pivoted and backhanded Bolan, rocking the chair and causing sparks to flash behind Bolan's eyes. "That's for trying to shoot my brother." He stalked out, leaving Bolan alone with the two mujahedeen.

"I apologize. That was uncalled for," Tuerto said, dragging Bolan's chair around.

Bolan spat a wad of blood onto the floor and shook his head to clear it. "Depends on your perspective," he said. He rotated his wrists, grabbing onto the back of the chair. A combination of age and the desert climate had weakened the wood. He couldn't break the chains, but if he had a bit of time, he could damn well break the chair. He needed to keep them talking and distracted.

"And just what is your perspective, Mr. LaMancha? Or should I call you, ah, what was it, Cooper? Is that your name?" Tuerto said.

"Is your name really One-Eye?" Bolan said.

Tuerto laughed. "Ha! No, no not really. Yes. There's little need for secret identities at this juncture, eh? Allow me to introduce myself, Mr. Cooper. I am Tariq Ibn Tumart."

"Berber," Bolan said. "You're a long way from home, Tariq." Splinters dug into his fingers as he worked at the wood.

"Ma'sa'Allah," Tuerto said, inclining his head. "'If you must wage war, wage it in enemy lands.'"

"Abd al-Rahman," Bolan said. "A wise man, for his time."

Tuerto's eyes widened slightly. "You're a well-read man, I see." He clucked his tongue. "Most disappointing. I have so little opportunity to discuss literature in my line. The *ghazi* are not big on books, save one. Isn't that right, Fahd?" The big man made a grunt of what might have been assent. Tuerto turned back to Bolan. "You see? I find it an almost painful irony that the warriors of God have so little appreciation for the words and poetry of those inspired by him."

"It's a sign of the times," Bolan said, speaking louder to hide the sound of the chair's back crumbling in his hands. "People think Cervantes is a type of quesadilla."

"Cervantes? I take it back. You have terrible taste in books," Tuerto said, stepping back. He frowned. "Who are you really?"

"The Man from LaMancha," Bolan said, smiling slightly.

Tuerto snorted. "Amusing, but I think not. Are you with Interpol?"

"They don't do enough tilting at windmills for my taste," Bolan said.

"It will go hard for you if you continue," he said, hands behind his back. "If you are not Interpol, then are you CIA? Are you FBI? NSA? How much do you know?"

Bolan said nothing. His muscles tensed, preparing. Tuerto nodded sharply. "I was hoping that you would make this easy for both of us, Mr. Cooper. But I have ever been disappointed by men like you." Tuerto snapped his fingers and Bolan felt something hard crash into the back of his skull.

He made the leap anyway, dizzy as he was. The chair snapped and broke and his fingertips brushed across Tuerto's throat. The mercenary stepped back, eyes widening slightly. His hands flashed, quicker than Bolan could follow in his current state, and the Executioner sagged to the floor, his body refusing to respond to his commands.

"We have a tried-and-true method of dealing with enemies with stubborn tongues in my country, Mr. Cooper." Tuerto sank to his haunches and leaned close. "We let them boil in their own sins."

11

Amira Tanzir watched from the stifling room she and the others had been forced into by Sweets's men. It had been a dance hall at one time but presently it was an empty wreck. Most of the windows had been painted over, but she was able to see out of one, though not by much. When the gunfire started, she almost leaped to her feet. She resisted the urge, however, and merely joined a few of the others at the window. Cramming her face against it, she had watched as her contact was surrounded by Sweets's followers, and a familiar icy fear gripped her heart.

She had been a part of more than one undercover operation that had gone wrong, and it always ended in blood and tears. She had hoped this one would go differently. Obviously, her hopes had been in vain. Her first instinct had been to help in some way. Her second had been to do nothing. Like a good agent, she had chosen the second. The mission came first. It always came first. But she still felt sick. She needed confirmation that she'd made the right call.

Turning her face from the window, she tapped the bead in her ear and murmured, "Control?"

A burst of interference greeted her. Then, "—eport," Control hissed.

"Agent James's cover has been blown," she said simply.

There was a moment of silence, and then, "Yours?"

"I'm still in place," she said, hating herself even as she said it. She should have at least tried to help. But, to what end? No. No, she had to focus. Only the mission mattered. Nothing else.

"Good," Control said. "You're on your own. Try not to get killed."

"What about Agent James?"

"He's not your priority. Tuerto is." Control fell silent. She heard the click of the line being closed a few moments later and she frowned. It was true, James wasn't her priority. She didn't have to like it, though. She sat and watched shadows move and dance and die on the walls, and wondered who was doing which of those acts at that moment outside. After a time, she slumped down, trying not to think of anything in particular.

"What do you think is going on?" someone said in a hushed voice. The gunfire had long since gone quiet, but no one had checked on them.

"Do you think it's the cartels?" a woman said, clutching her meager possessions closer to her. More voices spilled forth then as people began shouting questions and concerns at one another in growing fear. The climate of hysteria bubbled and frothed around Tanzir and her skin crawled at the naked confusion rising from the others.

She understood it completely. She had seen it before, in North African cargo containers, the holds of Libyan fishing boats and on Russian tankers. Men and women fleeing the bad and often ending up smack-dab in the middle of the worst. The world had grown too small to accommodate the desire for someplace better. Every country in the world was slamming its borders shut, out of fear or necessity. Sometimes the one amounted to the other. Yet people still tried to cross borders, rivers, mountains, oceans in pursuit of something approaching a better way of life.

Forced by circumstance to deal with criminals, whether they were coyotes or snakeheads or some other species of smuggler, the lucky ones made it to the so-called Promised Land carrying only a bit of hard debt. Others were forced to act as unwilling couriers for illicit goods or substances—guns, secrets, heroin, cocaine, everything under the sun—or to sell themselves to pay for their trip. She had seen men sign away their own organs to see to their family's safety, and women as young as twelve forced into prostitution to pay for a three-day ride in a cramped and stinking ship's hold.

Her knuckles went white as the shooting stopped. Silence fell, and the voices of the others fell with them. Ten agonizing minutes later, the door opened and a man stepped inside. Big, bigger than any man Tanzir had ever seen, with fists coated in dried blood. Animal eyes swept the crowd. "Settle down," he said, his voice strangely high-pitched for a man of his size. It was a little boy's voice, issuing from a brute's mouth. "Nothing is going on, everything is fine," he continued. His gaze fell on Tanzir, and her skin prickled and crawled at the naked lust she saw there.

She looked away, wondering whether he was one of those men for whom violence was an aphrodisiac. She wished she had a weapon, but was confident of her ability to procure one, if it became necessary. She forced her fingers to straighten, to droop. Tension was her enemy, as much as Tuerto.

The newcomer's eyes stayed on her for long minutes and then he wheeled around and stomped out, slamming the door behind him. She heard padlocks click into place and the jangle of chains. The coyotes weren't taking any chances.

Tanzir closed her eyes again, and settled back to wait.

JORGE'S HEAD SNAPPED BACK and blood spattered across the floor. The big Arab stepped forward and grabbed the man's hair, jerking his head forward before punching him again. Pain splintered James's thoughts, keeping him conscious despite his wishes. He was tied to a chair and his looks weren't so good anymore.

"That bullet wound looks like it hurts, Mr. James," Tuerto said from the room's sole piece of furniture, a busted-up bed.

The Berber lounged back against the wall, smoking a cigarette. "We can get you medical attention, if you simply answer a few questions."

"G-go to hell," James grunted.

"Fahd," Tuerto said. The fist smashed down, and the agent's jaw felt as if it had been caught in a car door. He nearly fell over, chair and all, but the big Arab caught the back of the seat and set him back up. "Fahd was a torturer, you know, for the Republican Guard. He doesn't talk much, but he is eloquent with his hands." Tuerto stubbed the cigarette out on the wall and pushed himself up with languid ease. "You are with the United States Border Patrol, yes? But not your friend Cooper, I think."

"Go blow," James said, grinning, his teeth red with his own blood. Again came the fist, this time in an uppercut that sent his teeth sawing into his own tongue. Gagging, he jerked back. A foot hooked the leg of the chair and righted him.

"Rude," Tuerto said. "Was this serendipity? Coincidence? Or are there larger forces at work?" he said, almost to himself. "Who are you working with, my friend?"

"Jack Bauer," James gurgled.

"I quite like that show. Hit him, Fahd."

Fahd did, again and again and again. Blows fell like raindrops, and James felt his face go loose like a bag of gravel.

"Your friend Cooper is dead," Tuerto said. "You do not betray him by telling us what we want to know. Not now."

James looked away. It was all the defiance he could muster. Tuerto sighed. "Fine. Fahd, make him talk. When you have what I need, kill him. Don't linger," he said, turning to leave. "Goodbye, Mr. James."

"Be seeing you, Tuerto," James croaked as the door closed. He looked up at Fahd and smiled gamely through split lips. "Now, let's you and I get acquainted, shall we?"

Fahd's only reply was a gap-toothed grin. Then, raising his fists, he began again.

TUERTO CLOSED THE DOOR and blew out a breath. Sweets was waiting for him, a sly smile on his face. "Not talking, is he? Ol' Jorge has unplumbed reserves of testicular fortitude, I'll give him that much, the lousy little backstabber."

"No, he is not talking. Neither is Cooper, bad cess to the man." Tuerto stroked his beard, thinking. "But until we know what they know, we cannot risk moving."

"Look before you leap, huh?" Sweets said. "I can dig it. It's gonna cost extra, though."

"What?"

"Extra. As in, 'money.' Cash preferably, but we'll take a money order."

"Our current arrangement suits me better," Tuerto said.

"How about that?" Sweets said. "Not me. Us, I mean." He waved a hand. Several of the surviving coyotes waited on the stairs, ostensibly not looking at them, but holding their weapons in such a way as to give lie to their indifference. Tariq felt a thin smile spread across his features.

"I have a hundred men."

"Little less than that, I think," Sweets said, his own smile staying in place. "Me, I got, what? Eight? Of course, all of yours are downstairs, but four of my guys are right *fucking* there, Mr. One-Eye." Sweets spread his hands. "Double or nothing, we stay on. You jerk us around, we leave in the one working vehicle. You and the beaners can eat each other for all I care. Or try to make it on foot. That desert will kill you faster than a bullet, Arab or not."

"I am a Berber," Tuerto said mildly. He glanced back at the door, then at Sweets. "Not an Arab."

"Same difference," Sweets said.

"Not to Berbers and Arabs," Tuerto said. He sighed. "Fine, it will take a day to make the arrangements."

"We got time," Sweets said. "Cooper fucked them trucks up but good."

"Cooper," Tuerto growled, fists clenching.

Sweets laughed. "Should just let Digger have him. Maybe you could learn a few things, watching him work."

"No. We have our own methods of punishment. Torture, for its own sake, has never appealed to me," the man with one eye said.

"Are you squeamish?" Sweets said.

"Merely efficient," Tuerto said, waving a hand. "Butchery should be left to butchers, as the saying goes. Now, if you'll excuse me," he went on, stepping past Sweets.

"Where are you going?"

"Taking our Mr. Cooper to his final resting place," Tuerto said without turning around.

12

Bolan knew that it was much later when he opened his eyes again. He did so with reluctance, not to mention some difficulty. Dried blood cracked and flaked down his cheeks as he glared up at the sun. Every limb and joint was aching and throbbing, his skin tight, and there was a red heat creeping up behind his eyes. Even his hair hurt, right down to the roots. He licked dry, cracked lips with a tongue that felt as if it was wrapped in steel wool, and tested the nylon cords that held his wrists and ankles flat against the unpleasantly warm surface of the roof of the stripped and gutted hulk of a car.

There was no telling how long he had been there in the middle of the desert, nor did he remember the trip. The only things he recalled were fists and feet and rifle butts working him over like an overenthusiastic butcher wielding a meat tenderizer as Tuerto left the room. He wondered how long he'd been unconscious. Head blows were bad news, and the aftereffects could crop up when you least needed them. Blinking against the light, he took in his situation.

Arms and legs spread, Bolan was at the mercy of the elements. There was sand in every crevice and his throat was as dry as the ground. Bruises and contusions were already forming on his bare torso, and he was finding it hard to breathe. He closed his eyes and pushed the pain aside, trying to organize his thoughts. But the sun beating down on his head like a hammer and the bone-deep pain that riddled his battered body made any clear thoughts difficult.

"Well," he croaked, "this is another fine mess you've gotten me into." His comment was swallowed up by the desert, answered only by the distant cry of a bird of prey. If Bolan had believed in omens, he might have wondered about that. Other things occupied his mind at the moment, though. Like the fact that the rusted roof was fast heating up and his skin was beginning to burn.

Fighting to control the instinctive urge to thrash, Bolan tested each limb, first legs and then arms, pulling on his bonds. The nylon bit into his sweaty flesh like smooth teeth. His eyelids felt hot, but he kept his eyes closed, trying to ignore the orange spots dancing through the black of his vision. With a grunt of effort, he twisted his shoulder joint until it creaked, rotating his right wrist until his fingers could tap the top of the car's door frame. The nylon had been threaded through the busted-out windows, leaving him spread-eagled on the roof.

His fingers, dangerously numb, clawed at the door. If he could find a shard of glass or a loose flake of metal, anything with an edge, he might be able to cut his way free. He had to stop after his shoulder began to complain. A spasm spread through his abused body like ripples in a lake, and he took a minute to rest.

"They really did a number on you, old man," he grunted softly. His stomach lurched and he tasted bile. Images of his stomach acids beginning to bubble and turn to gas in his belly filled his head. He tried to work up enough spittle to wet the inside of his mouth, but there was none to be had.

His fingertip brushed something painfully sharp and drew a hiss from him. A twist of splintered metal, probably created during whatever accident had left this wreck in its current condition. Unfortunately, he couldn't quite reach it. Thinking quickly, he took a long breath and shifted his opposite shoulder. It dislocated with an unpleasant sound and Bolan couldn't manage to restrain a sharp cry. A coiling pain slithered up and down the limb as the twitching fingers of its twin fastened around the shank of metal and pulled on it. With the extra bit of reach the dislocation had granted him, he managed to jerk the shank free, though it cut his fingers to the bone. Shifting the sharp twist of metal through his blood-slickened fingers, Bolan brought the far tip against the cords fastened around his right wrist. Breathing heavily from pain and effort, he began to saw at the nylon.

The skin on his back tightened as the car roof began to sizzle. He sawed as fast as he dared, gashing his wrist more than once. The strands of nylon began to fray and spread like the head of a hydra. He imagined he could smell meat cooking and growled deep in his throat, a sound of frustration and defiance.

Many times in his career the Executioner had been close to death. The hornet-kiss of a bullet, the scorpion-sting of a blade or the sweaty grip of a strangler's hands had all brought him down to the shores of the Styx, but he'd never yet crossed over, and he'd be damned if he'd do it in this fashion.

The twist of Detroit steel dropped from his bloody fingers and he almost howled. His body bucked as every square inch of skin burned. With a convulsive heave, Bolan jerked at his bonds, thrashing, hoping he'd cut deep enough into the cord.

He heard the sound of something popping and realized that it was the few remaining threads of nylon. He tore his right arm loose and sat up as the tension on his left arm immediately went slack. He groaned as his skin peeled away from the car roof. He fumbled at the knots around his left ankle and worked them loose after several long minutes. Legs free, he rose up and immediately rolled down the front of the car. He hit the hood hard enough to jar his dislocated arm. He yelped and crashed onto the ground in a brief flurry of dust.

Breathing hard, he lay there for a while, his blood pooling around him, his thoughts rattling around in his head like shards of broken glass. After a short time, his good hand reached up and his fingers curled in the car's grille. Slowly, painfully, Bolan pulled himself up onto his knees. Breath whistling in and out of his nostrils, he pressed his left shoulder against the hood. Then he whipped it back and smashed his shoulder into the front of the car. It took two more tries to put his shoulder back into its proper place and Bolan gave a yell with each attempt.

Weakly, he lurched to his feet, his body trembling. His blurring vision caught sight of the shard of metal he'd used to cut his wrist loose and he scooped it up, nearly falling over in the process. Swaying, he looked around. He caught sight of the saguaro stretching dumpy limbs toward the sun above and staggered toward it.

He needed water. A bird fluttered out of the cactus, startled by the apparition looming over it. It shrieked and rose into the air, wings humming as Bolan nearly collapsed against the cactus. It rose nearly higher than his head and he eyed its spines with apprehension. It was bigger than he'd thought, and more fragile looking. He'd heard about people killed by collapsing cacti, crushed beneath their spines. In his current debilitated state, he wasn't sure he could trust his reflexes to do their job properly.

But there was no option B. No door number two. It was find water immediately or most certainly die later. And Bolan didn't intend to die here.

He looked back at the car. The slender shape of tire iron was visible in the dirt beside its back wheels. Bolan dropped to his haunches and excavated the rusty tool. He crammed the metal into the socket and turned back to the cactus. If he could puncture it, there'd be water inside. It was a felony to damage one of them, but he'd worry about that after the threat of death by dehydration was taken care of.

Behind him, the car creaked. Bolan stopped and glanced over his shoulder. A black king snake slithered through the scrub brush. Bolan waited, counting, his every sense extended to its limits. When nothing revealed itself, he turned back to the saguaro.

The sound of delicate padding reached his ears a moment before he heard the rumble of the jaguar's growl. He spun, but saw nothing, save a flash of black rosettes splashed across tawny fur. The spiky shrubs shifted and whispered as the animal moved through them. It was in no hurry. Bolan couldn't bring himself to be insulted.

The Sonoran Desert was the only place within the boundaries of the United States that the big cats were found, and they were running close to being endangered. In other circumstances, Bolan would have done everything he could to avoid the animal and give it the run of the land. But this wasn't other circumstances. He glanced down at his bloody hand and grimaced. The smell of blood had likely drawn the cat.

He turned slowly as it circled him, never quite letting itself be seen by its intended prey. Bolan fought the atavistic urge to flee that threatened his ragged composure. He was in no shape to outdistance the animal, and he'd rather face it than have it behind him anyway. His grip on the tire iron tightened.

Bolan knew that if the jaguar came at him, he'd have to dispatch it quick. If the animal got its claws or teeth into him, Bolan's chances for survival were on the sharp edge of nil. He swung the tire iron, trying to loosen up his protesting muscles. Adrenaline flooded him, but it wouldn't be enough. He was barely on his feet as it was.

"Walk away, pal," he said hoarsely. "Go look for dinner somewhere else."

The only reply he got was the sound of the animal moving through the brush. He caught the flash of a tail out of the corner of his eye, and the animal chuffed. Green eyes met his and Bolan froze, hoping not to provoke it. The eyes broke contact a moment later.

Bolan began to get a clear idea of why the cat was taking its sweet time. It was moving slowly and awkwardly, as if it was hurt. Some farmer had taken a potshot at it perhaps, or it had gotten caught in a trap. Regardless, it was looking for slower prey than rabbits.

The sound of his blood dripping onto the thirsty soil was loud in Bolan's ears, louder even than the thump of his heart. He wondered, almost idly, if the jaguar could hear it. Did it sound like thunder to its sensitive feline ears?

Metal squealed beneath wicked claws as the cat abruptly scrambled up onto the roof, seemingly unconcerned about the heat. Tail lashing, it gazed at Bolan with interest. A wide tongue lathered its chops and its eyes were bright with hunger.

It wasn't the first time he'd seen eyes like that, or, rather, an eye. He wondered how far he was from the town with no name, and the man called Tuerto. Mr. One-Eye, the man who'd beaten Bolan down and left him to cook under the Sonoran sun. Tariq Ibn Tumart, the man who had taken Bolan's ally and who had likely killed him, despite Bolan's best efforts.

"But my best wasn't good enough," Bolan snarled. He let the tire iron slide through his fingers until he was gripping the end. He'd get one swing, he knew, just one. "So it had better be good, right?" he said harshly, his dark gaze meeting the cat's own. The jaguar snarled and Bolan's lips skinned back from his teeth.

"Come on then, pal. You want me? I'm not going anywhere," he said. Tuerto thought he was dead. And maybe he would be. But he wouldn't go quietly or easily.

The jaguar paused, as if confused by his tone. Then its muscles bunched abruptly, and its tail went rigid. Bolan tensed. The cat sprang, a death machine built over the course of millennia, designed and streamlined by evolution into a tawny thunderbolt. And the Executioner, a man not far removed from the beast facing him, his body honed into a weapon second to none, lunged to meet it.

13

Tanzir opened her eyes as she heard the chains on the door rattle. It was light outside, the sun spilling through the gaps in the boarded-over windows. She shifted, stretching lithely, one muscle group at a time. The doors opened and food was brought in—loaves of grocery-store bread and bologna, and a bucket of water. People crowded around, shouting questions, but not too loudly. The coyotes ignored them, save for the leader, Sweets, who raised his hands and grinned like a naughty schoolboy.

"Folks, I do apologize about the accommodations and the disruption to your itinerary, but it could not be helped. Safe to say, we are going to be on our way this fine day, if nothing else serves to distract us." His eyes shifted through the faces, settling on Tanzir. "Some of you faster than others, I will admit."

Her heart beat faster. Had Agent James talked? Had he even seen her? Recognized her? Adrenaline flooded her weary limbs and she fought to control the sudden surge of panic. Sweets trotted toward her and she prepared to strike, her muscles knotting in readiness.

"Ain't you a pretty one?" he said, dropping to his haunches in front of her. He rubbed his chin and grinned. "Guess I can see why he likes you…."

Tuerto. He must mean Tuerto. She relaxed slightly, looking at him through lowered lashes. She said nothing, waiting for him.

"After last night, he needs to work off a bit of frustration.

Get up, girl," Sweets continued in Spanish. He snapped his fingers and she rose obediently. He smirked and looked at the others, eating as if they hadn't done so in days, and then he looked back at her. "Guess every batch of raisins got one grape in it, huh?" he said in English.

He led her out of the building and across the street. In the hot light of day, the town looked worse. There were unpleasant stains congealing in the dirt of the street. Here and there, bodies lurked under tarps and moth-eaten bedsheets. A truck and van clung to one another like lovers, a building slumping over them. Someone had tried to give the town a makeover, Tanzir noted. Perhaps she hadn't given Agent James enough credit.

Sweets saw her looking and clapped a hand on her shoulder. "Now, don't go getting distracted, sweet pea. You got a big day ahead. Yes, indeed." She stopped herself from peeling his hand off her, one broken finger at a time.

The building had once been a bar. These days it was a den for two-legged scavengers—Tuerto's men. They were hiding from the oppressive gaze of the sun, and watching her with avaricious intent. "Just up the stairs, sweetness," Sweets said, patting her rear. "He's waiting for you up there. Fairly salivating, he is."

She took the stairs slowly, as if hesitant and unsure. It wouldn't do to appear too eager when she saw Tuerto. Infatuation could turn to suspicion fairly quickly. Her palms were sweaty and the boards sagged beneath her feet.

He was waiting for her at the top of the stairs. But it wasn't Tuerto. She could hear him panting, and her hackles bristled. "Hello," he said in his little boy's voice.

She stopped, saying nothing. She glanced back down the stairs. Sweets waited at the bottom, arms spread to either banister. He looked at her knowingly, and she felt like a lamb fed to a lion. She looked back at Digger and essayed a smile.

He held out a hand. She took it gingerly. He was sweaty, and she could smell the nervousness bleeding off him. "You're pretty," he murmured, stroking her hair. His touch sent a thrill of revulsion through her, but she continued to smile.

"Come on," he said. "I want to show you something real nice…" His hand grasped hers with a spasm of strength, and he led her toward a door. "Real nice," he said again, opening the door.

The room was almost spartan in its bleakness. A bed that had seen better decades and a set of drawers that hung crookedly. Dust covered everything, and the room smelled hot and unpleasant. A trained observer, she spotted the telltale spatter of what was likely blood on the old wooden floorboards. It was still sticky.

"I only ever saw it once," he said, seating her on the bed. "But I been looking for it ever since. Here and there, you know. Django helps, when he can, but mostly it's me." He looked at her almost guiltily. "He's never seen it, so he doesn't know. I want to show him, but…" He trailed off and shrugged.

"Show him what?" she said. He started.

"You can talk American?" he said wonderingly. Big fingers stroked her hair. "I ain't never known one as could yet. Maybe you are the one."

"The one what?" she said, conscious of the strength in those fingers. She reached up and took his hand and he shuddered. He jerked his hand loose and stepped back. Both hands went behind his back and he smiled like a baby seeing its mother for the first time.

"The one who's going to show me the black bird," he said as he revealed the wide-bladed KA-BAR knife he'd been holding behind his back.

TARIQ STEPPED OUT of the jeep in a swirl of dust. They'd had it hidden behind one of the buildings when Bolan began his destruction of the trucks, so it had escaped his attention. Tariq slapped the burning metal of the hood and laughed a clear, light sound. Abbas glared at him. "Why are you so happy?" he snarled. "We still know nothing about him!"

"And so? By the time his people, whoever they are, look for Mr. Cooper, he will be a strip of cooked meat. A fitting punishment for a man who tried to subvert Allah's will, eh?"

"We should have shot him," Abbas insisted. "And the other one, as well!"

"Abbas, we cannot shoot everyone," Tuerto said. "More, I tire of it. You are a traditionalist, man. You should appreciate what we just did!" He spread his hands. "A more fundamental death I cannot imagine."

"I can! It involves a bullet!" Abbas said, yanking at his beard. His mad-hawk eyes jittered around, seeking possible complaints. "We should leave today."

"And how would you do that? Where would you go? Do you know how to slip over the border undetected? Do you even know where the border is?"

Abbas fell silent, but his glare spoke volumes. Tuerto sighed. "Complain all you wish, but my plan is still sound. And when you kneel before Allah, you will know I was right."

Abbas stomped away, grumbling under his breath. The mercenary watched him go and shook his head. Abbas was becoming more of a problem every day, in every way. Something might have to be done about him, and soon. Tuerto was loath to dispose of tools, but needs must. He shrugged and looked around the town.

A dusty flyspeck, much like the one he'd grown up in. Granted, the one he'd grown up in had never felt the sting of a cowboy's spurs.

"Feh," he murmured. "Mr. Cooper. You are swift, but not swift enough." He turned back toward the desert, and wondered idly if the big American had woken up yet, and if he had, what he was feeling…was the man frightened? Or was he attempting to free himself? Or was he dead already, from the dozen and one hurts they had levied on him?

"Ma'sa'Allah," he said to himself. Smiling, he made for the building where their "camouflage" was being held. He'd made certain that food and water was brought to the captives, as well as blankets and other comforts, insomuch as a pesthole like this had them. There was no reason to treat them like cattle. He could sympathize with them, in truth.

They wanted a better life, just like peasants the world over. They wanted to be safe, to have full bellies and to be free of the overseer's whip. There was no sin in that.

It was a shame that most of them would die before achieving that goal. He stroked his beard. He had ordered that they be spared, but, he knew his men were not all so inclined to listen. Abbas, for one. It was a waste of bullets, but they would do it nonetheless, so assured of their passage into paradise, that a few extra infidel souls would not weigh their consciences down overmuch.

A few would listen though, and would feel much the same. America was their enemy, not a ragged peasant seeking to pick strawberries.

Thinking of that, however, put him in mind of the woman. Her face swam before his eyes, still so familiar, but he couldn't say why. She seemed more intelligent than the run-of-the-mill border rat, but then, who could say why people ran one way or another. Some of those in that group were just as likely to be doctors and lawyers as well as fruit pickers or day laborers. He wondered what she was.

"Maybe I should ask her, eh?" he said to himself. Decided, he ambled toward the building. He was, by nature, a hopeless romantic, he knew. A girl in every port, with two in every city. He liked women more than he ought, and found their company infinitely preferable to that of men.

One of the coyotes, Eddie, he believed the man was called, was sitting outside the doors, nursing a warm beer. He looked askance at Tuerto. "She ain't in there, Sheikh."

"What," he said, stopping. "Who?"

"That piece of ass? She gone."

"Gone? Gone where?" Tuerto said, a premonition bristling across his mind. "Sweets," he said before the other man could answer.

"One of them, yeah," Eddie said, rising from his seat. He emptied his bottle and slung it against the building. "I hope you weren't too fond of her."

Tuerto turned and sprinted for the saloon.

THE KNIFE WAS NOT A SURPRISE. Tanzir had read the files on the men involved, and more, she had read between the lines. This sort of profession attracted the sadistic sorts, the sexual predators and the brutalizers of women. It was a profession of power over the powerless. No, the knife was not a surprise.

Digger's speed, however, was. She caught his grasping hand and her thumb found the bundle of nerves in his wrist, jabbing it and rendering the paw numb. He yelped, more in surprise than pain, and the knife swept out faster than she could follow. It slid across her cheek like a kiss and Tanzir fell back onto the bed. Her feet shot out, mule-kicking into Digger's manhood. His yelp became a strangled moan and he bent double. He uttered a rasping gasp, as if he was about to be sick and she took the opportunity to jump over him and race for the door.

A hand tangled in her hair, yanking her back with almost neck-cracking force and she slid across the splinter-laden floor and slammed hard into the wall. Digger, breathing hard, glared at her with something approaching religious fervor.

"Don't want to come out, do he, that old black bird? But I'm gonna see him, damn for sure," he breathed, the big knife spinning in his hand. "I can hear him rustling between your ribs." He dived on the last word, the tip of the knife digging for a point between her breasts. She rolled aside and the blade gouged the wall. Her leg swept out, the sole of her feet cracking against his ear and sending him tumbling.

She'd had enough training to know that if he got his hands

on her, she'd be dead. No fancy tricks or nerve strikes would be enough to compensate for his raw strength. Tanzir had to get out, to get away from him before he got a permanent grip on her. She just needed a distraction....

There was yelling from below, and then the rush of feet on the stairs. Digger paused and turned, like a wary animal. She tensed, preparing to move.

The door slammed open and nearly fell off of its hinges as Tuerto's foot connected with it. The pistol in his hand cracked and the knife in Digger's hand went flying in a serpentine curl of crimson. Digger shrieked like a child and stumbled, clutching his hand.

Tanzir took the opening, diving past Tuerto and out into the hallway. It was easy enough to play the terrified rabbit, what with the adrenaline thundering through her. Tuerto glanced at her, and then turned his attention back to Digger. The big man's hand was bleeding, but not damaged seriously. The bullet had cut through the web of flesh between his thumb and finger before lodging in the wall. He swung his head like an angry buffalo and took a hesitant step.

"No," Tuerto said. "This is the second time I have almost shot you. Do you want it to be the last?"

"Put that gun down!" Sweets snarled, stalking up the stairs, his pistol clutched in one steady hand. "I swear to the Lord Our God Jesus Hisownself, if you so much as twitch, I will blow you to hell, Mr. One-Eye!"

"Your brother will be there to open the gates for me, Sweets," Tuerto said icily.

Sweets's demeanor abruptly changed. He held up his hands. "Now, hold on, hold on, maybe we're getting a bit ahead of ourselves here. Said some heated stuff. Waved guns around, no reason we can't come to terms, I think."

"The original price," Tuerto said.

"What?"

"We will no longer be paying you double," Tuerto said, not looking at Sweets. "The original price stands, yes?"

"I—" Sweets began, face coloring.

"I am comfortable with death. Is your brother?" Tuerto said.

"Django?" Digger said, looking at his brother.

"Fine!" Sweets snapped. "Fine, damn you!"

"And the girl, of course," Tuerto said. Tanzir didn't know whether to feel relieved or insulted. He did not look at her as he stepped back.

"No," Digger said.

"Yes, fine," Sweets said, waving the larger man silent.

"And there will be no replacements, eh?" Tuerto said.

Sweets's face had assumed a placid look. "Fine. I'll keep him on a short leash while we're here," he said, glancing at his brother, whose hands clenched into meaty fists. He looked back at the man with one eyed. "I said it before, but you're awful squeamish for a fellow planning to blow up nursery schools."

"There is a difference between war and murder, Mr. Sweets," Tuerto said, holstering his pistol. "I admit that the line is a fine one, sometimes, but it is there nonetheless."

14

Bolan knew that he'd blown it, even as the tire iron whistled through the air. The jaguar tumbled to the side, its lunge aborted by Bolan's own. The tire iron missed it by inches and Bolan was forced to stumble back as the cat clawed at him. With its snarl rippling in his ears, the Executioner gripped the tire iron in both hands and took a batter's swing.

The tire-iron connected with the jaguar's outthrust paw, and Bolan heard bone snap. The animal shrieked and spun in a circle as Bolan tried to stay out of its way. Limping, the jaguar began to stalk him as he backed away. Exhaustion crept through Bolan, and black spots danced across the surface of his vision. Even if the cat was hurt, it still outmuscled him, especially given his current physical state. Even adrenaline could only keep him on his feet so long.

The jaguar's tail lashed and it circled him, its eyes blazing intensely. Bolan followed it, turning slowly, his stomach heaving and his head spinning. The tire iron felt as if it weighed a hundred pounds and the round head dipped as Bolan's arm began to shake. But iron nerves strummed and Bolan raised his improvised weapon, forcing his sluggish muscles to respond through sheer will.

"Sorry, pal, there's no such thing as a free lunch," Bolan said hoarsely. The jaguar growled. A moment later it charged, kicking up a cloud of dust. Bolan fell backward and rolled aside as the cat scrambled through the space where he'd been standing. Even as the cat turned, Bolan shot to his feet and brought the tire iron down, hoping to connect with the animal's skull.

He caught the cat a glancing blow on the head and it screamed and fangs fastened on his wrist with bone-crushing force. Bolan couldn't contain a scream of his own as the tire iron tumbled from his grip. His shoulder burned as he yanked the cat around. His free hand snagged it by the ruff and, body protesting, he rammed its skull into the car, denting the metal.

The cat released his wrist and went limp. Bolan dropped the jaguar and fell to his knees beside it. His chest was heaving like a bellows and sweat covered him. The animal was still breathing and might rouse at any moment. Cradling his bleeding wrist, he scrambled toward the tire iron. Even as his fingers touched the tool, the jaguar gave a querulous grunt and rose up onto three shaky legs, its head hanging low.

Bolan scooped up the tire iron and rolled onto his back as the cat turned and started toward him again. It sprang at him, crashing into him even as he sat up. Its hot breath washed over his face as he battered at it with the tire iron.

Suddenly, the cat stiffened and slumped, its weight pressing down on him. Bolan rolled it off and straddled it, raising the tire iron. He noticed the dart sprouting from its leg at the same moment he heard a shotgun being readied.

"Drop it, mister," someone said. Bolan let the tool fall. "Now stand up. And do it slowly."

"Wish I could oblige you," Bolan croaked. He got off the jaguar and fell heavily onto his back, his vision blurring. He heard voices, but at a distance. And then everything went black as the world crashed in on him.

When he awoke, the black was replaced by the gleaming white of a hospital room. Bolan tensed, and felt a stab of pain, first from his arm and then from everywhere. With a grunt, he made to sit up.

"Easy, fellow," someone said. "Easy does it."

A strong hand on his shoulder helped him up. Bolan looked

at the hand's owner. A square grin greeted his examination, nestled in a craggy face the color of baked clay. Dark eyes returned the favor. "That cat tore you up but good, my friend."

"I was in bad shape before he got there," Bolan said, rubbing his shoulder. The man was stout and built like an inverted triangle. His salt-and-pepper hair was cropped almost painfully short, and he wore a tan shirt and dusty black denims. "What happened?" Bolan asked.

"I was going to ask you the same thing. Someone shot that cat with a load of buckshot and I was out seeing to it. Nothing worse than a pissed-off jaguar with a hide full of iron, especially since it's part of my job seeing that no one kills one of them. Or vice versa, come to that. I caught it with a tranquilizer dart right before she gave you a lobotomy with them teeth of hers."

Bolan flashed back to the sight of the jaguar's teeth looming over him, and the smell of the carnivore's breath and added the memory to the pile of close calls he'd endured throughout his long war. "Thanks. If I can ever return the favor…"

"Yeah, about that…I'm Joel Watts, chief of police for Tapowo, and I was thinking I might have a few more questions for you, if you're feeling up to it." Watts pulled a tiny notebook and a stub of pencil out of the breast pocket of his uniform shirt and set them down on the bed.

"And if I'm not?" Bolan said.

"I'll ask anyway, but you'll enjoy it less," Watts said, smiling. "See, usually we don't find folks strapped to cars out there. Now, we might find them wandering, or in a gulley, or on the side of the road, if they make it that far, but never, at least in my time, strapped to a car, as it appeared that you were, if we are to believe the evidence."

"Glad to hear that I'm special. Where's Tapowo?" Bolan said.

"Here, or hereabouts," Watts said, gesturing. "We're in the local clinic."

"Free?" Bolan asked, looking around.

"Veterinary, actually," Watts said, looking slightly embarrassed. "Tapowo is too small for a proper hospital. You got to go up to Tucson for that. We make do with the horse doctor. Your sparring partner is in the room next door."

"Glad to hear it," Bolan said.

"You actually sound like you mean it," Watts said. "Mind telling me what you were doing on our property, beating up on our animals?"

"Who's 'our'?" Bolan said, feeling as if he'd come in halfway through a movie.

"This is all Tohono O'odham land, friend," Watts said. "It's not much, but we call it home." Bolan recognized the name, though only vaguely. A southwestern Indian tribe, with a reservation that actually sat on both American and Mexican territory; a fact which had caused them no small difficulty in recent years as border conditions grew harsher. "Care to tell me why you were in our backyard?" Watts pressed.

"Not really."

"Shame. Maybe I should have left you for the damn coyotes. They travel in packs out there big enough to bring a guy like you down without breaking a sweat," Watts said. "Why were you out there?"

Bolan slumped back. "How long was I out?" he said, avoiding the question.

"Six hours, give or take. You took a pounding," Watts said. "How about a name…"

"Cooper. Matt Cooper. I'm with the Justice Department," Bolan said. Six hours. Dark thoughts pried at the lid of his composure. God alone knew what could happen in six hours. He might already be too late. His mind shied away from the thought. He sat up again. "I've got to get out of here."

"You're not going anywhere, not until we figure out what you were doing out there," Watts said, taking hold of him, albeit gently. "Just lay back."

"No," Bolan said. "There's no time." Chain rattled and he looked down at his bandaged wrist. It was handcuffed to the examination table. He shot a look at Watts, who sat back and shrugged.

"I don't take chances with fellows who can down a jaguar with his hands."

"I had help from a tire iron. Chief, you've got to let me go," Bolan said intently. "There are some very bad people out there planning to do some very bad things, and they've got friends of mine as prisoners." He rattled the cuffs. Friend, anyway. If Tanzir was smart, she was laying low. But James…

"You've been beat up, burned, baked raw and gnawed on by a cat, Mr. Cooper. I'd be remiss in my duty as a law enforcement professional if I let you go now." Watts picked up his notebook. "Tell me what's going on, and I'll put in a call to the tribal council, see what they say."

"I'd rather you call my bosses," Bolan said.

"I bet you would. But this is Tohono O'odham land and we don't intend to let the Feds back in if we can help it. It didn't work out so well last time," Watts said. "Talk, Cooper. Why were you out there? Who did that to you?"

Bolan slumped back. "Call my bosses. I'll give you the number."

Visibly frustrated, Watts stood and stuffed his notebook back into his pocket. "Is that the way you want to play this?"

"Only card I got, Chief," Bolan said. He rattled off a number. Watts left in a huff, and Bolan lay back. Eyes closed, he meditated, trying to push his hurts aside and clear the medicinal fog that coiled about his thoughts. He hadn't wanted to antagonize the chief, but he knew what awaited him down that road. Confirmation and double confirmation, answers leading to more questions as his story was filtered to any one of a number of federal agencies, none of which might be in the loop where the joint Interpol/border patrol operation was concerned, but all determined to be, even at the expense of botching the whole thing.

It wasn't, Bolan reflected, that the people who staffed those agencies weren't competent individuals, but the bureaucracy that they worked within was far too limiting for them to accomplish what needed doing in the time necessary to do it. People died while forms were filled out in triplicate and secretaries shuffled paperwork.

He dozed for longer than he'd intended, and when he snapped back to full wakefulness, he was keenly aware of the passage of time. He heard the yowls of cats and the cries of birds and dogs and remembered that he was in an animal clinic.

Well aware that there was likely a man on guard, Bolan leaned over and grabbed the railing that he'd been cuffed to. It took more effort than he liked to bend it out of shape enough to slide the cuff free, but he did it. They'd left him his pants. Filthy as they were, Bolan shrugged into them, laced on his boots and moved stealthily to the door.

If he could get to a car, he could make his way...where? He was reasonably certain he could find the town where Tuerto and the others had been hiding, but there was no guarantee that they were still there, even though he'd disabled almost all the vehicles. And it wasn't likely that anyone still there would talk to him.

That wasn't even taking into account his lack of weapons. He grimaced. He'd have to improvise on the fly. One way or another, he'd take them down.

Gently, he eased the door open, but saw no one on duty. If Tapowo was as small as Watts had intimated, he might not have left a guard after all. Or, there might be three.

Even as Bolan stepped out into the hall, the three men in suits saw him and started to hurry forward. The closest reached for him even as he opened his mouth to speak. Bolan didn't give him the chance, snapping his hand out to grab the newcomer's wrist and bend it back even as he jerked the man forward and thrust him face-first into the wall, rattling it hard enough to send a notice board clattering to the floor.

The second man came at him, displaying at least a passing familiarity with something approaching martial arts training. Bolan slid under the punch despite the protestations of his muscles, and gave his opponent a quick rabbit punch in reply.

The click of a government-issue Glock was loud in the hallway. Bolan straightened, frowning. He turned to face the third man, who aimed the weapon at him from several feet away.

"Who the hell are you?" the federal agent barked. "Answer me!"

15

"You saved me," Tanzir said in Spanish, trying to sound grateful. She sat with Tuerto in the room he'd commandeered for his use, stroking the front of his shirt.

"Of course I did. But I haven't even learned your name yet," he replied in the same language. He took hold of her chin and made her face him. "So…what is it?"

"Alma," she said.

"Alma," he said, rolling the name around in his mouth. "That is a pretty name." He dipped his head for a kiss, and she pulled back. He snorted. "No, I suppose not. Not after what you've been through." He rolled off the bed and stood, walking to the sink. He rinsed out two plastic cups and filled them with water, offering one to her. She took it gladly and gulped down the water greedily. She hadn't realized just how thirsty she was.

"I knew that there was something wrong with him the first time I saw him. He stinks of blood and madness. Like a tiger that's been lamed." He tapped the side of his head. "He is sick, up here. So is his brother, but his is a more common madness, I think." He sniffed. "Still, *Ma'sa'Allah*."

"As God wills it," she said.

He nodded, smiling. "Yes, exactly. As God wills it. We work with what we have." He drained his cup and set it aside. "A dancer, perhaps?" he said.

"A dancer?" she repeated.

"You, I mean. Were you a dancer? Your movements were

elegant, despite the situation. It was something involving co-ordination and agility, surely. A *vaquero,* perhaps?" he said, sinking to his haunches in front of her.

"I was a…policewoman," she said haltingly.

His eyebrow quirked in surprise. "Oh?" he said.

"Yes," she said, using her best rueful smile. She spread her hands. "I made some mistakes, you know?"

"Oh, yes, I know," he said, nodding. "Would one of those mistakes be why you are now smuggling drugs for the cartels?"

She allowed her features to tighten. "Yes," she said quietly.

He smiled. "I like a woman with character."

"How much do you like me?" she said.

"Oh, very much indeed… What are you planning to do once we cross the border, Alma?" he said, eyeing her intently.

She shrugged and leaned back. His smile grew. "Ah, yes," he said. "I see. Would you like to go with me, Alma?"

"Where?" she said.

"Canada, I think. It has been some time since I visited friends there, and I would not stay within the borders of the United States for all of the tea in China, I think." He stroked his beard, looking at her contemplatively. "Such a trip is always more enjoyable with…company, shall we say? And there is no company better than a lovely woman."

Canada, she thought. They had known he wasn't planning to stick around; Tuerto was an organizer, not a terrorist. He was a consultant in the field, but not a practitioner, as Control had put it more than once. Canada made sense. Tuerto wouldn't stop after he crossed the border, he'd simply head for the next as quickly as possible, to be out of the United States before the inevitable occurred.

"You are not staying in America?" she said, trying her best to sound confused.

He looked at her. "No. This country holds no pleasure for me." He smiled crookedly. It was an almost charming expression, if you hadn't seen a similar look on his face as he shot an informant. She had been several miles away that time, watching him through a satellite feed. The men sent to capture him had been minutes too late.

"I have always wanted to visit Canada," she said. He smiled and stroked her cheek. She wanted to bite him. The door rattled as a fist pounded on it. Tuerto snarled and turned toward it.

"What?" he snapped. "What is it?"

"Open up!" someone shouted. "I want to talk to you!" Tanzir recognized the voice as belonging to one of Tuerto's men, the thin one called Abbas. "Open up, Berber!"

"It is a punishment, is it not?" he said, looking up. "Oh, Allah, why do you inflict these devils upon me, your faithful son?" He looked back at her. "Up. Back to your accommodations you go."

"But…" She hesitated, looking for some excuse. Something was going on. "What if the big one comes back for me?" she said, seizing on the question.

"He won't, but if you wish, I shall post one of my men to watch over you. They need to stay alert anyway," he said calmly, chivying her toward the door. The other man was still knocking, and Tuerto stepped past her and jerked the door open, allowing Abbas to stumble into the room. The man stopped himself before he fell, but recoiled comically at the sight of her.

"Filth!" he barked.

Tuerto swatted Abbas's head. "Be polite." He turned to her. "Come, I will see that you are escorted safely. Never fear, Alma, my dear."

"We don't have time for this—this playacting! Fahd thinks that American is finally ready to talk!"

Agent James! Tanzir fought to keep her face from showing her shock. She had assumed the worst, and thought that he was dead. But if he wasn't, he could still blow her cover. Panic flared and then guttered out, stamped down by determination.

If Agent James was still alive, then she could make up

for not helping him earlier. And she could take Tuerto in the bargain.

Tuerto closed the door on Abbas, shutting off the man's diatribe as effectively as if he'd hit him a second time. He led Tanzir downstairs and motioned for one of his men, a young Afghani, to follow. "This is Yusuf. Yusuf, take Alma back to the others and stand guard, hmm?"

Tuerto grabbed him by the shoulder and leaned close, murmuring quietly. The young man nodded, his eyes narrowing. Yusuf led her away, and she didn't look back. She was too busy planning a rescue.

When she was back inside the building where the others were being held, a few people quietly asked questions, but most ignored her. No one wanted to become involved in anyone else's problems, and if she was unlucky enough to have attracted the coyotes' attentions, well, it was too bad for her. Tanzir knew that this was less callousness than survival instinct, but it still made her long for an ending to the whole charade.

She looked around the old dance hall. It had been used to store more than just people in its day. Tarpaulin-covered hills abounded against the back wall. Most were likely empty boxes and crates or broken furniture from better days gone by, but there might be something useful in there, nonetheless. As she drew close, she realized why no one else was back here. The stink was strong, and her eyes watered. It was a familiar odor, however. Following her nose, she pulled one of the tarps back and smiled. A dozen gasoline cans sat stacked in a rough pyramid. She pulled the tarp fully aside and knocked on them, hoping to hear even the faintest slosh. Several minutes later, she calculated that there was enough left to enact the plan forming in her mind.

She sank down and rocked on her heels, thinking. She reached up to touch her communications link, but then let her hand drop. If she contacted Control, they would order her to sit tight. But if she did that, she ran the risk of being discovered once Agent James was forced to talk, and of him dying as well.

Neither option held an especially pleasing prospect. She stood and stretched, turning toward the others. "Does anyone have a lighter?" she asked.

JAMES SWALLOWED BLOOD and wondered whether Cooper had gone out the same way. They hadn't mentioned the big man again, and he knew it was likely because he was dead. James had liked the Justice Department agent, though he'd only known him for a day or so, and guilt for not dissuading him from joining him nestled in his belly.

The man had dealt himself in to help, but had only wound up getting killed trying to save James's hide. He'd thought that if things were going to go bad, it would have been Cooper's fault. But instead, his own hubris had brought him low, just as his momma had warned him so many times before.

How long had Sweets known? Had they found out about Agent Tanzir, as well? James hoped not. He hoped the woman from Interpol was still safely hidden in plain sight, or, failing that, a long way away.

Outside, someone screamed. It was a terrible sound, long and high-pitched enough to make James's teeth itch at the roots. It sounded like a soul in torment. At the first warble, the big Arab slapped James, knocking him over. The chair cracked and split as it struck the floor, but Fahd didn't notice. There was shouting outside on the street, and James could smell smoke in the one nostril that wasn't full of dried blood.

The agent feigned being stunned. He was in what was likely the worst shape of his life, with bruises forming on bruises and things inside him rattling around like marbles in a tin can. Through the slit in a swelling eye, he saw a jagged splinter of wood separate from the chair and skitter across the floor.

Hope flared within him. The chains were loose and he slipped an arm out and clawed for the splinter as if it was the last rung on the ladder to paradise. As Fahd stooped and peered out the window, James got to his feet, splinter in hand. With one swift motion that he knew he'd regret later, he grabbed the man's beard from behind and rammed the splinter up through his back.

Fahd gave a surprised grunt and James sawed the strip of hard wood up, angling it just so. The big man shuddered and then slumped. An exhalation of breath escaped his lips as James lowered him to the floor.

Thinking quickly, he squatted. "Ha," he said, finding the pistol holstered on the dead man's hip. He pulled it free of its holster and checked the magazine automatically, then the slide. It was an old Beretta, but well taken care of. "Small miracles," James said. He looked out the window. Smoke was rising steadily into the bright blue sky.

Pistol held down by his side, James eased the door open. There was no one in sight. He took a moment to let his strength build. Every limb felt loose in the socket, and his muscles felt like wet taffy.

It was a long shot, but if he could make it to one of the vehicles, he might be able to get clear of the town and get help.

TUERTO WAS ARGUING with Abbas when he heard Yusuf scream. The cry spiraled up and up and up, piercing the ears of everyone within sounding distance. Both men ceased arguing and began to run, heading for the stairs.

"That was Yusuf!" Abbas said, clawing for his weapon.

"I know!" Tuerto snarled. It was the coyote again, he knew it. He knew it! Red visions of what he would do to the oversize brute filled his head as he raced through the saloon and out into the street. He skidded to a stop as he saw what awaited him—Yusuf staggered toward him, wrapped in a shroud of flame!

The Afghani screeched like an animal as he extended his arms pleadingly. Then he sank to his knees and fell flat, wreathed in the stink of burning meat. Tuerto had seen bad deaths before, but this one…he wrestled down the bile that threatened to crest over his palate and grimaced as the smell reached him.

"What the hell is that?" Sweets said, skidding to a stop nearby.

Tuerto growled and hauled his pistol out, swinging it toward the coyote. "You! You filth of the world! No more chances! Now you die!"

16

"Easy," Bolan said. "We're all friends here." He raised his hands and stepped back, putting the two agents he'd downed between him and the barrel of the pistol pointed at a spot directly between his eyes. Everything about them screamed Fed, and Bolan had had enough encounters with their kind to know that a false move could get him dead as quickly as a jaguar's bite.

"Hell with that—Stop moving!" the agent barked.

"I'm stopped," Bolan said, reflecting that he was in the absolute last place he wanted to be. The two men on the floor were getting up, albeit slowly and groggily. "What's this about?" he said, already knowing the answer. Watts had obviously made a call, though possibly not the one Bolan had hoped he'd make. It had sent up flags, and men had been dispatched to take him into custody. Whose custody, however, he couldn't say. It didn't matter, in any event. Bolan wasn't planning to go into custody. Not when there were lives at stake—lives depending on him.

"Shut up!" the man with the gun snapped. "Yeovil? Adler? You guys okay?"

"They're fine," Bolan said. "My name's Cooper. I'm with the—"

"I said shut up!" the gunman said. "Get on your knees. Now!"

"No, I don't think I'll be doing that," Bolan said. His eyes swiveled, taking in the gun butts protruding from the rising men's shoulder holsters, and then the fire extinguisher on the wall. If he went for the guns, there was a good chance someone would get shot. But the extinguisher... Bolan spun, snapping a kick into the closest man, sending him staggering back into the gunman. The pistol went off, tearing through the chipboard ceiling. Bolan ripped the extinguisher off the wall and turned it on, blasting all three men with foam.

"Sorry, boys, I hate to do this, but needs must," Bolan said, emptying the extinguisher. Sliding forward across the slippery floor, he jammed the end of the canister against the hands holding the pistol and dislodged it, snapping it up before it could hit the floor. Then with quick, athletic movements, he sprang over the tangled men and headed for the door, the pistol in his hand.

If he could just get to their car, he could—

"Drop it," Watts said, pressing his gun to Bolan's head even as the Executioner bolted out through the doors the Federal agents had entered through. The police chief had been waiting on the other side. "Drop it nice and slow, Mr. Cooper, and I won't have to add to your list of woes. Neither one of us wants that, do we?"

"Maybe not, but they certainly do," Bolan said, nodding back toward the men he'd downed. The agents were on their feet and charging at him, blood in their eyes. Bolan grinned and tossed the pistol down, stepping back as the trio bulled through the doors.

Watts eyed them, and the barrel of his pistol drifted toward them nonchalantly. "You three guys feel like identifying yourselves?"

"Carter, FBI," said the one who'd drawn down on Bolan. He pulled a badge out of his sopping coat and flashed it. "We're taking this man into federal custody..."

"Bull puckey. He's my prisoner until the tribal council says different," Watts said. "Now, get them guns out of my face, or I'll get twitchy."

"Chief Watts, this comes from directly on high—" Carter began.

"I don't care if it comes from Jesus, Buddha or Allah, Agent Carter," Watts said. "Settle down or I'll settle you down." He glanced at Bolan. "You, too, Cooper." He jerked his chin at the handcuffs dangling from Bolan's wrist. "You're paying for that examination table, by the by."

"I assume you called the FBI?" Bolan said.

Watts shrugged. "Probably somebody higher up than me on the local food chain, but until I hear what's what, nobody is taking anyone in my custody anywhere."

"Look, we've got a warrant. This man has information on a sensitive matter," Carter said, frowning. He glared at Bolan. "We need to know what he knows. It's a matter of national security."

"On that, I agree," Bolan said. "I'll talk to your bosses, but not until I've made a phone call." And not until I know for a fact that they—and I—haven't already screwed things up beyond all repair, he thought.

"No phone calls, I think," someone said. Bolan and the others turned. Several men in suits stood in the doorway of the clinic. The one who'd spoken turned his attention back to the cell phone he cradled against his ear. "We've found him, Control."

Bolan detected the slightest accent curling around the man's words. "Interpol," he said, not looking at Watts.

"Very good, Agent…Cooper, was it?" the man with the phone said. The suit was Italian, but the accent was Gallic, if Bolan was any judge. The phone was clicked shut. "You will come with us, yes?"

"No!" both Watts and Carter barked simultaneously.

Bolan crossed his arms. "I'm not going anywhere, with anyone, until I make a phone call."

"Don't be stubborn, Agent Cooper. Time is of the essence," the Interpol agent said. He jerked his head and the three men who'd come with him moved forward. Two of them wore border patrol windbreakers. All three were armed.

Bolan tensed. Then, abruptly, he relaxed. There was nothing for it. "Fine, I'll go."

"We'll all go," Carter said, stepping forward and snapping a pair of handcuffs onto Bolan. Bolan didn't resist, not wanting to waste any more time. Watts, however, protested.

"Hey, now, if anyone is cuffing him, it'll be me."

"Sorry, but you're sitting this one out. The Federal Bureau of Intelligence thanks you for your assistance in apprehending this man. But, frankly, you can shove off now. Get back to rousting drunks or whatever it is you do out here," Carter said brusquely.

Watts frowned. "That's it, huh?"

"That's it," the FBI man said. Watts looked at Bolan, who gave a slight smile and shook his head. Watts squinted, and then nodded, rubbing the back of his head.

"Guess I've been kicked out of the circle, huh?"

"Trust me, the air is better out here than in there," Bolan said, seething inwardly but trying to present a calm face. He moved toward the door, followed closely by the border patrol agents and the dripping Feds. Hopefully, Watts had taken his meaning. If not, Bolan was in for a long day.

"You do not care for our company?" the Interpol man said, falling into step with Bolan. They left the building and Bolan squinted at the rising sun. He'd lost a day, possibly two. He couldn't lose any more time. If that meant he had to play nice with the big boys, then he'd simply have to do so.

"Not the company, but what it means," Bolan said.

"Ah. Red tape, you mean," the other man said. "My name is Chantecoq, by the by. I am Amira Tanzir's direct superior."

Bolan looked sharply at Chantecoq. "You've heard from her?"

"Not since yesterday. That is why you are in custody, Cooper." Chantecoq looked at him through the lenses of dark glasses. "I want to know where my agent is. And what you have done with her."

Bolan fell silent and looked away. A pretty face swam to the surface of his thoughts, but he pushed it aside. Guilt was a useless sort of balm in situations like this, especially when no one was truly at fault. "Not me," he said finally.

Chantecoq smiled blandly. "No? We shall see."

There were two black SUVs waiting for them outside. Bolan was motioned into the first, and Chantecoq and Agent Carter climbed in after him. The FBI man glowered at him as he employed wadded handfuls of paper towels to clean the fire-retardant foam from his suit.

"You shouldn't have pulled your gun," Bolan said.

"You shouldn't have thumped my partners," Carter said.

"Be fair, he did not know who you were," Chantecoq murmured. He looked at Bolan over the rim of his sunglasses. "Then, we do not know who he is. Just who is Agent Matt Cooper, Justice Department, answerable to?"

"I have a number you can call," Bolan said.

"So you keep saying." Chantecoq's gaze moved over to Carter. "I find it interesting that he showed up at a critical point in our operation."

"Not ours," Carter said. "Or did you forget that you decided not to mention your little sting to the Bureau?"

Chantecoq made a flippant gesture. "FBI, NSA, BPA, so many letters, so little time."

"I'll give you a letter, you—" Carter began.

Bolan cleared his throat. "May I ask where we're going?"

The two men looked at him as if suddenly remembering his presence. Chantecoq rubbed his chin. "We set up a temporary headquarters near the border. We'll take you there and debrief you."

"You aren't debriefing anyone until we get our people down here!" Carter snapped. "You don't get to play around on American soil and not follow proper procedure, mister."

Bolan sat back as they continued to argue. Under different circumstances, it would have been funny. But every cross word and harsh look was another minute wasted while evil men carried a cargo of death toward innocent Americans.

"El Tuerto doesn't care about procedure," Bolan said.

Chantecoq looked at him sharply. "What do you know about Tuerto?"

"I know that his real name is Tariq Ibn Tumart," Bolan said. "He's a Berber. He's been classically educated. And he's less interested in martyrdom than money."

Chantecoq sat back, a speculative look on his face. "That's... quite a bit, actually. More than we know, in fact. How did you come by this information?"

"Simple," Bolan said. "He told me."

Carter laughed. Chantecoq frowned. "Why would he do that?" he said.

Bolan shrugged. "He thought I would be dead before I could tell anyone."

"Guess he misjudged you, huh, Cooper?" Carter said, grinning. "It seems like you put everyone on the wrong foot, not just us."

"It's a flaw," Bolan said. The Fed nodded appreciatively. Chantecoq said nothing, simply examining Bolan silently for the remainder of the ride. The agent was a tough egg, Bolan could tell. He wasn't a desk jockey, and his concern for Tanzir was palpable. Bolan felt some sympathy, but not enough to say anything else.

He needed to cut through the red tape, to get everyone moving in the same direction at once, if they were to prevent Tuerto's plan from succeeding. And that meant forcing them to do what he wanted. It wasn't often that Bolan pitted his will against those of monolithic bureaucracies, but it was a fight he was certain he could win. There was no man alive more stubborn than him, when the need was great enough. He just hoped it wouldn't take too much time.

The drive was a short one, all things considered, though Bolan's impatience made it seem far longer than it truly was. As they pulled into the base camp, Carter was already on the phone to the Tucson office of the FBI.

Bolan got out even as a number of men in ties and windbreakers hurried forward out of the large military-issue tents that made up the camp. One of them waved a walkie-talkie in Bolan's face. "I don't know who you think you are, mister, but you've got a hell of a lot of explaining to do!"

"And I'm happy to do so," Bolan said. "But on my terms."

"What the hell does that mean? Chantecoq?" The man looked at the Interpol agent.

"I don't know," Chantecoq said. "He insists on making a phone call."

"Great! Sure! Why not? Let's get more people involved, see how far we can push this leaky boat before it sinks!" the man snarled. He threw a cell phone to Bolan. "Call whoever the hell you want, as long as you tell me where those damn coyotes are holed up and where our people are!"

"My pleasure," Bolan said.

17

Tanzir felt a twinge of guilt as the man burned. The look of surprise on his face would stay with her for a long time, if she survived this day. It had been a simple enough matter to fill a few empty soda bottles from one of the crates with the dregs of gasoline and dollops of oil and machine grease from another box, and then stuff them with rags, creating something approaching Molotov cocktails.

The improvised mixture had exploded over the man as he opened the door in response to her pleading, and his scream had rattled her more than she cared to admit. She stiffened her resolve, knowing that he had planned worse fates for innocents over the border. Innocents who would live, thanks to her actions; it was a cold comfort, but it was all she had.

She had three more of the bottles, and as she scuttled out into the daylight, she was already wondering where they would do the most damage and be the most distracting, to enable her to see to Agent James's rescue. Running between the buildings, she slung one beneath a boardwalk, where it struck an exposed water pipe and burst. Flames licked greedily up the side of the building from beneath.

Two left. Holding the bottles by the necks, she hurried forward. No one had seen her yet, being far too busy watching Yusuf burn. She skidded to a stop and saw the trucks. Men moved amongst them, obviously working at repairs. She had wondered why they hadn't moved out yet; she had assumed

Tuerto was simply being overcautious. Instead, it appeared as if someone had put a thorn in their collective paw.

A man turned and saw her. Eyes widening, he began to yell. She sprang forward, her bare feet kicking up dust as she cocked her arm back and threw. The bottle bounced off the startled man's chest and struck the open hood of the truck he was standing next to. The fire spread quickly through everything under the camouflage netting that had been erected to protect the vehicles from prying eyes.

As she prepared to lob her last bottle, a wide hand swatted it from her grip. It hit the ground and burst, exploding into fragments. She dived aside, twisting to avoid the flaming liquid. A heavy boot stomped down between her shoulder blades, pinning her flat to the ground.

"Hello, little bird," Digger said, forcing her down as she tried to squirm out from under him. "I been missing you, sweetness. Django!" he called out, turning slightly. "Django, I got her!"

Tanzir thrashed beneath his weight. But he was too heavy to dislodge. She had to make him move. Straining, she reached out and grasped a shard of glass and, twisting her body, she jammed the glass piece into his leg. Digger yelped and stumbled off her, kicking her in the side as he moved. She crawled to her feet, clutching the glass.

"Drop it, little lady," Sweets said, aiming his pistol at her. Fire crackled behind her, and smoke wound between the buildings. He glanced back at Tuerto, who was following him, looking slightly shell-shocked. "I told you she was a spitfire," he said mockingly. "And next time you threaten me will be the last, Mr. One-Eye," he continued, his grin becoming a glare.

"Alma? I don't..." Tuerto began, looking at her, his one good eye wide in disbelief.

"He tried to force himself on me!" she said, pointing a shaking hand at Digger, who was clutching at his leg. "He tried to—"

"Quiet," Sweets said conversationally.

"I could almost believe that if I hadn't seen the professional way you set those fires," Tuerto said and glanced up at the flames curling into the painfully blue sky. He shook his head in apparent admiration.

Sweets whistled. "Yes, sir, very neat. That is some spec ops bullshit right there, ain't it, boys? Cooked up some goddamn weapons of mass destruction right there in that building…" He lifted his pistol. "Guess Jorge and Cousin Frank weren't the only foxes in the henhouse, were they?"

Tanzir took a breath and tightened her grip on the chunk of glass bottle. If she could reach him before he—

"Don't," Tuerto warned, interrupting her thoughts. "I don't know who you are, woman, but I quite like you. I'd hate to shoot you."

"I wouldn't," Sweets said, licking his lips. "Or we could just let Digger have her, like I wanted to do in the first place."

"No. I want to know who she's working for," Tuerto said.

"Does it matter?" Sweets said.

"It does indeed," Tuerto snapped, turning to glare at the other man. "At every turn we are beset with traitors and obstacles! Does it not strike you as curious that we are so afflicted?"

"Nope. Shit happens. Let's shoot her, dump her in a gulley and get to figuring about how we're going to salvage this shit, huh?" Sweets said.

Ignoring him, Tuerto turned to Tanzir. "Who is it? The Mexican government? Interpol?"

"Yes. And you're under arrest," she said, raising her jagged blade of glass. She aimed it at Tuerto. "You have no idea how long I have waited to say those words." She took a single hopping step and sprang for him, the glass hissing as it split the air. But Sweets was faster, however, lunging forward from the side and swinging his gun butt down on her skull, dropping her senseless to the dirt.

"Interpol's got them a funny idea of arresting folks if that's how they do it," Sweets said, looking down at her. "Little filly went right for your throat, One-Eye, like you smacked her momma."

Before Tuerto could reply, a burst of gunfire caused them all to turn. "Now what?" the man with one eye said.

JAMES FIRED, catching the man in the chest and sending him rattling back down the steps. Carefully stepping over the body, he retrieved a second pistol and headed for the door. Someone was setting fires. Halfway down the stairs, he heard screams and smelled burning meat, and he began to wonder what was going on.

Bullets plucked at the banister, snapping him back to the here and present. Falling back against the wall, he pulled both triggers, replying in kind. Someone screamed downstairs, but more weapons opened up in counterargument, sending splinters of wood spattering against his abused frame. James nearly fell headlong down the stairs as he moved as quickly as possible to the ground floor.

His pace was reduced to inches by a combination of pain and sporadic gunfire. He caught sight of heads bobbing behind the bar. Through blurry eyes, he saw the ancient chandelier swinging in the hot breeze. Tipping backward, he fired at the ceiling. The decoration gave way with a shrill squeal. It shot downward, crashing into a table and setting up a cloud of dust that mingled with the smoke.

James followed it, nearly sliding down the remaining stairs to the floor, and threw himself behind a table, knocking it onto its end with one stiffening shoulder. He ignored the blazing streaks of pain that radiated through him and concentrated on the bar.

He fired at the bottles behind the counter, sending a shower of alcohol and glass down on the men behind it. Someone shot to their feet and James shot him. Then he ran for the door, his back itching, expecting to feel the kiss of a bullet at any moment.

The heat of the day washed across him, drying his sweat where he stood. Shapes rose up before him and he fired, both pistols jerking in his hands. Another body tumbled.

"Christ on a goddamn crutch! You ain't killed him yet?" Sweets said. James wheeled, following the sound of his voice. Sweets stepped back, raising his weapon. Tuerto and the others halted in their tracks, watching the confrontation.

"You know us half-breeds, Sweets…tougher than goddamn cockroaches," James croaked, his throat as dry as sandpaper. He was thirsty, and the guns felt like lead weights in his hands. He heard feet behind him and he stepped forward off the porch, hurrying toward Sweets on legs as wobbly as noodles. "Don't move! Nobody move!" It was such a surprising maneuver that his command was obeyed instinctively by everyone present.

"Somebody shoot him! Shoot him!" Sweets yelped, backing away. He made to fire, but the proximity of James's weapons to him made him hesitate. He knew he was good enough to plug the agent, but was he good enough to do it before James did the same to him?

James saw those thoughts flash across the surface of Sweets's mind and he smiled grimly. "You might kill me, Django, but I'll sure as hell take you with me. Tell them to back off! All of them!"

"Crap," Sweets said, letting his weapon drop. "Everyone chill out. Let's none of us be hasty at this here juncture, huh?"

"There is hasty, and then there is hasty," Tuerto said, not lowering his weapon. Neither did any of his men. "Cost and reward, Mr. Sweets. Which is worth more? Your life? Or Agent James's?"

"I'm thinking mine!" Sweets said as James sidled behind him.

"Start backing up. And you stay where I can see you, Digger!" James shouted hoarsely. The big man froze like a wolf caught in a security light. "We're taking whatever's got wheels and is still working and we're getting out of here, Sweets."

"Got your tail between your legs, huh, Jorge?" Sweets said.

"Damn straight," James said. "A good coyote knows when to run, Sweets. You taught me that."

"Going to leave your partner behind then?" the rangy coyote said nastily. James froze.

"Cooper?"

"Nope," Sweets nodded. Tuerto gestured and two of his men brought Tanzir forward. She hung between them, head bowed, hair covering her face. "Figure you two knew about each other, right?"

"Almost certainly they did," Tuerto said, pressing the barrel of his pistol to the woman's head. "Interpol has been after me for years now. Though they've never dangled bait quite like this before."

James took a breath. "Let her go," he said.

"No. I think not," Tuerto said, cocking his weapon.

"I'll kill Sweets!"

"And so?" Tuerto said.

"Thanks," Sweets said.

"Shut up!" James snapped. "I'll kill him. Let her go."

"It is a matter of cost and reward, as I said, Agent James. She is worth more to me than him, I'm afraid," Tuerto said simply. He shrugged. "It is as Allah wills it. Shoot and then die yourself. Or surrender and perhaps live a day more. The Garden of Forking Paths has narrowed to but two, for you, my friend."

The border patrol agent hesitated. The sun pounded down on him like a hammer, the heat searing the top of his head, and his vision was spotted with splashes of crackling white. Tuerto was right, he knew. Killing Sweets was a useless gesture, satisfying as it would be. Tuerto was more dangerous. And he held all the cards.

Tanzir looked up blearily, and their eyes met. She mouthed the words *shoot him,* and he wondered whether she meant

Tuerto or Sweets. It didn't matter. At the moment, he knew he couldn't hit the broad side of a barn. He was beat, barely able to stand. His pistol barrels dipped and he blinked.

"Hell," he said.

"Smart man," Sweets said, spinning and slamming a fist into his belly. James gasped and sank down, but not far. Sweets grabbed his hair and drove a knee into his chin, knocking him flat onto his back. "You're more intelligent than I gave you credit for, Jorge. Pity it led you here, huh?" He kicked the pistols away, stomping on one of James's hands in the process. The agent was too out of it to do more than grunt as the bones in his hands grated together.

Sweets sank to his haunches and leaned close, looking more lupine than ever. "Going to wish you'd been stupider, Jorge. Going to wish you ran. I promise you that."

18

Outside Tapowo

The helicopter dropped to the ground in a cloud of dust, sending men and women scrambling to cover sensitive equipment and prevent papers and maps from being blown away. Bolan watched it land and fiddled with the cuffs that still bound his wrists.

It was an easy enough thing to get them off, but left on, they made a point. The call had been quick, and as Bolan had hoped, the cavalry was immediately en route. Watts hadn't let him down. The stocky tribal policeman had been just irritated enough to do as Bolan had hoped, and made the call to Hal Brognola.

The latter was the first man off the chopper, his ever-present cigar caught between lips thin with frustration and barely repressed fury. He stumped forward, his head lowered with bulldog stubbornness, and met his opposite numbers in the dust and the wind of the chopper's descent.

The man in charge of the border patrol contingent was Greaves, and his opposite number, the German named Rittermark. Both men looked ready for a fight, and were thus surprised when Brognola stepped past them and stopped in front of Bolan.

"Striker, you look like shit," he said.

"If it's any consolation, I feel worse," Bolan said.

Brognola snorted. "It's not. Take those cuffs off, huh? It's embarrassing."

"Just waiting for you," Bolan said, slipping the cuffs off with practiced ease and tossing them to Chantecoq. The Frenchman looked at the cuffs, and tossed them to the Fed, Carter.

"I believe that these are yours, *non?*" he said. Carter grimaced.

Bolan stood, rubbing his wrists as Greaves and Rittermark stormed into the tent after Brognola. "Satisfied, Cooper?" Greaves said. "Feel like talking now, maybe?"

"Maybe you should watch your tone," Brognola said without turning around. "Well, Striker?"

"I'm good. Did you get in touch with the Mexicans?" Bolan said.

"After an eternity on hold, yes. They're mobilizing as we speak."

"The Mexicans?" Greaves said, sharing a look with Rittermark.

"Si," a heavyset man said who'd followed Brognola off of the chopper. No one had noticed him, intent as they were on other matters, but presently all eyes were on him. Round and wearing a military uniform, he tucked his hat under his arm and nodded to Bolan.

Bolan grinned. "Hello, Ortega."

Felipe Ortega was not quite an old friend, but he was close. It was he who had alerted Bolan to the Sinaloa poppy field that he'd destroyed earlier in the week. Ortega was no friend to the cartels, and he was happy to hurt them in whatever fashion was at hand, including passing information he couldn't act on to certain heavily armed, possibly insane, from his perspective, *gringos.*

When Bolan contacted Brognola, the man had literally sputtered in relief. Brognola had feared the worst when Bolan had broken contact to go to Agent James's aid and hadn't gotten back in touch. When Bolan had finally been allowed to make a call by Greaves and Rittermark, Brognola was already been en route to Arizona from the Wonderland on the Potomac.

After talking with Bolan, he'd immediately called Ortega, Stony Man's contact in the Mexican government. And Ortega, for his part, hadn't been happy to learn that the help he'd given to Interpol had been repaid with an information blackout concerning a hundred armed terrorists on his patch. And he said as much even as the helicopter's rotor blades slowed enough to allow him to speak without shouting.

"We were disappointed to learn that we were being kept out of the loop on a matter of such…international urgency," Ortega said, looking around the camp. "When we helped you insert your agent into the situation, we assumed you were simply looking to plug the flow of heroin traveling through American ports. It took a phone call to inform us otherwise."

"Brognola…" Greaves snarled.

The big Fed held up a hand. "Not just me."

"It was Jorge—Agent James," Bolan spoke up. Ortega nodded.

"Indeed. Though his warning didn't reach us until far too late, I'm sorry to say." Ortega looked at the others. "There was a certain amount of interference."

Rittermark grunted. "Your organization leaks like a sieve, you mean. That's why we kept you out of it. No reason to embarrass your government."

"Yes, how kind of you," Ortega said blandly. "But that particular leak has been plugged, you'll be glad to know."

"What do you mean?" Greaves said.

"Agent James's contact," Ortega said. "He passed what James told him up the line. And when Mr. Brognola called us and told us what was going on, we found out where that information had stopped." He clenched a fist. "Then we simply plugged the leak." He looked at Bolan. "Thanks to Agent Cooper here, we have eliminated a prominent gap in our security apparatus." He smiled broadly. "The least we could do, then, in return, is to mobilize what forces we have near the border for a, ah, training exercise." He looked at Greaves. "Feel free to inform your superiors. Unlike you, we feel little need for secrecy."

Greaves flushed. "Mexican sovereignty wasn't violated," he said tersely. "Besides which, the bad guys aren't on your patch anymore."

"No, but you were quite rude," Ortega said. "And they are lurking in the no-man's-land between our two countries…that makes them both our responsibilities, to my way of thinking."

"This is very amusing, but what exactly do you mean by a 'training exercise'? Need I remind everyone that I still have an agent in play?" Chantecoq spoke up, his voice growing heated. Bolan looked at the Frenchman, reappraising him.

"Has she reported in?" Rittermark said.

Chantecoq hesitated. "No. Not since yesterday."

"Then, I am sad to say, we must assume she has been discovered," the German said bluntly. "Even as Agent James was, unfortunately."

"Hey, he had some help on that score, if I recall correctly," Greaves snapped, glaring at Bolan.

"Playing the blame game isn't going to get anything done," Brognola said, speaking over everyone with a practiced parade-ground bark.

"Agreed," Rittermark said sharply. "If the Mexican government is mobilizing, then we must assume that Tuerto will make a run for it."

"You think he'll abandon his mission?" Bolan said.

"No," Chantecoq said, speaking up. "No, he will simply adapt his plan. We know that he intends to leave his men before they begin their attack, wherever and whenever that is scheduled. He will follow through with that part of it, at least."

"He's a jackal in a trap," Rittermark said.

"Sweets will run, too, if he's got the capability. Deal or no deal, he'll move like his ass is on fire if he sees tanks on the horizon," Greaves said, gesturing to Ortega.

"But Tuerto won't let him leave without him," Bolan said. Upon learning One-Eye's true identity, the Interpol agents had managed to put together a surprisingly comprehensive file on Tariq Ibn Tumart. Reading it, Bolan was struck by the similarities between himself and the mercenary. Algerian by birth, Tuerto, or Tumart, had become involved with the Berber Arouch Citizens' Movement and had apparently lost family, as well as an eye, in the Black Spring Disturbance of 2001. After that, he had seemingly resurfaced as a terrorist-for-hire, ostensibly pitting himself against the sorts of men he blamed for his family's deaths.

"What do we know about this Sweets?" Ortega said. "Could he be pressed into turning your man over to us?" He looked at Rittermark. The latter glanced at Greaves, who frowned.

"Maybe…" he said doubtfully.

"No," Bolan said. "I've met Sweets. He's a rattlesnake. There's no telling which way he'll strike."

"If our people are still alive, they might try to use them as bargaining pieces," Chantecoq said.

"Or kill them," Carter said. It was the first thing the FBI man had said in some time. Bolan looked at him, considering. Then he looked at the helicopter that had brought Brognola and Ortega.

"How many of those can we get?" he said, pointing.

"What? Why?" Brognola said. "What are you thinking, Striker?"

"I'm thinking that we take a page from Tuerto's playbook," Bolan said. "While Ortega's people are keeping them busy, we hit them hard and fast from the air. We can keep them off balance long enough for someone to get your people out, and to get Tuerto in custody."

"Someone?" Brognola said, smiling. "You mean you, right?"

"I owe it to them," Bolan said simply. "I can get into the

town and keep Agents Tanzir and James pinned down long enough for the cavalry to arrive. And I can make sure that neither Tuerto nor Sweets manages to weasel out of our trap."

"Now wait a minute…" Greaves began. "Why don't we just—"

"What? Argue some more?" Chantecoq said. Rittermark shot a glare at his subordinate, but nodded sourly.

"Our original plan has been compromised, obviously. We must adapt. How long until your people hit the target?" the German said, looking at Ortega. The big Mexican rubbed his chin.

"Probably nightfall, give or take."

Bolan stepped out of the shade of the tent and looked up at the sky. Squinting, he calculated against the position of the sun. "Then I've got maybe three hours." He looked back at the crowd of suits. "I'll need gear."

"We don't even know where this town is!" Carter said.

"Of course we do," Bolan said. He looked at Chantecoq and Rittermark. "I assume you've already triangulated Agent Tanzir's position from her last communication? Just in case?"

Chantecoq looked at his superior, and then nodded. "Yes. Though the odds of them still being there—"

"Are pretty good," Bolan interjected. "I managed to damage most of their transportation. There's no way they're getting all those men out of that town, and both Tuerto and Sweets damn well know it, which is why we need to get James and Tanzir out of there ASAP."

"Sounds good to me," Carter said. The FBI agent patted his pistol. "When do we leave?"

"We don't," Bolan said firmly. "I do. As much as it pains me to say it, we need to keep any more potential hostages out of the bad guys' hands."

Carter flushed. Bolan knew how the agent felt, but he didn't allow himself to feel pity. He looked at Brognola. "I'll need gear…"

"In the chopper," the big Fed said, smiling slightly. "Kissinger says hello, by the way."

"Tell him I love him, too," Bolan said, smiling bluntly.

"What do you intend to do?" Greaves said. "Are you planning on taking on a whole town of *mujahedeen* by yourself?"

"Not for long, if things go according to plan," Bolan said. "Granted, things haven't been going according to plan so far, but I trust you gentlemen can make it work. You'll have to." He began to walk toward the helicopter.

Chantecoq caught up with him. "You're in no shape to do this, Cooper. Not by yourself."

Bolan looked at him. Despite his words, he knew the Frenchman wasn't so much concerned with him as with someone else. "I'll keep her safe," he said.

Chantecoq blinked and stepped back. "What?"

"Amira," Bolan said softly. He put a hand on the other man's arm. "I'll make sure she gets out of this alive."

Chantecoq's cheek twitched, and he seemed to want to say something. Instead, he simply nodded brusquely. Bolan nodded back and climbed aboard the helicopter. It took off a moment later, carrying him back into the desert. Ignoring the variety of aches and pains that plagued him, Bolan began to gird himself for war.

19

"It is a shame you had to kill Fahd. I quite liked him, despite the odor," Tuerto said, looking down at James. His men had tied the border patrol agent to the bed, and his skin was going an unhealthy gray. Stress and his wounds had robbed him of vitality, but his eyes flickered.

"S-sorry," James croaked.

"Yes, well…" Tuerto pulled up a chair. "Your value has diminished substantially, my friend. You're probably wondering why I'm keeping you alive, hmm?"

James didn't answer. Tuerto sniffed. "In truth, I am keeping you around merely to annoy Mr. Sweets. He is rabid for your death. Amazingly, I think your betrayal personally affronted him," he said. He looked at the agent and nodded. "I know. I am shocked, as well."

He rose. "You live because you are still useful to me, as a hostage, if for no other reason. I have been at this long enough to feel a noose closing about me. I may soon need bargaining chips."

So saying, he left James alone in the room and went out into the hallway. He paused, scratching his eye socket. He could still smell smoke on the air, and recognized it for the portent that it was.

"Things fall apart, the center cannot hold," he murmured. "The falcon must fly," he continued, paraphrasing. He chuckled bitterly. Failure was not unfamiliar to him. He had had operations blown out from under him before, but familiarity did not impart enjoyment.

He needed to see to his escape, and soon. He walked down the hall, toward the room where they were keeping Alma— no, Amira Tanzir. A surge of anger cut through him. Maybe Sweets's feelings concerning James weren't so shocking after all…betrayal was never pleasant.

It had taken some time, but he had finally recalled why her face was familiar. He had seen her once, in a little market town. Presumably she had been with the Interpol team sent to apprehend him before he set off the explosive device he'd planted in a certain man's bag.

The man had been the leader of a terror cell; ineffective and awkward, he was to be disposed of to make way for a more dynamic leader, a service which Tuerto had been only too happy to provide, considering the paycheck involved. Like many organizations, al Qaeda felt it necessary to keep a bit of distance between itself and internal assassinations. It wouldn't do to be seen sanctioning the killing of the Faithful, even if it was in good cause.

He'd seen Agent Tanzir in the crowd minutes before he'd set off the device, and had been struck then by her beauty. Just two ships passing in the night, he'd thought. Instead, she'd been an iceberg he'd narrowly avoided.

"Twice now, in fact," he said out loud. He paused in front of the door. There was a murmur of voices inside. The smoke had indeed been an omen. His holy warriors were growing restless. He opened the door and stepped inside.

"We should kill the bitch," Abbas was saying, looking at the woman tied to the bed. "If she is in the pay of our enemies, she deserves to die!" The others in the room nodded solemnly. Tuerto closed the door behind him and cocked his head.

"You are not a gambler, are you, Abbas?" he said, causing heads to turn.

"What?" Abbas snapped, turning to look at Tuerto.

"Would you dispense with a bargaining chip out of spite?" he said, sitting on the edge of the bed. Tuerto looked at the woman. She was either unconscious, or doing a very good impression of it. "Or is it because she's a woman? Is your misogyny so virulent that it blinds your reason?"

"What?" Abbas said again, blinking.

"I said that you are an idiot, Abbas." Tuerto tapped the side of his head. "A fool. She works for Interpol, yes? Then she is worth more to us alive at this juncture than dead. The same as the man."

"Who says?" Abbas snorted. "Your plan crumbles as we speak, Berber. We will follow you no longer, I think. You have proven yourself to be less than competent."

The man with one eye frowned. "Have I?" He stood. "You mean, I assume, that it is my fault that you idiots allowed an American agent to convince you to shoot at our drivers and kill several of them? Not to mention lose a number of our own men in the ensuing incident? Or is it my fault that I managed to prevent you ungrateful dogs from killing each other in your fear that we had been betrayed? Or, perhaps, you're referring to the fact that I managed to convince Sweets and his remaining men, men who have no reason not to simply bugger off and leave us stranded, to stay and continue on despite the aforementioned incident?" Tuerto threw out his hands. "You're right, of course, Abbas. Do forgive me. The levels of my incompetence are obvious even to the dimmest of us. Please, by all means… take charge." Tuerto turned to Abbas. "That is what you want, correct? To be in charge? To lead our holy warriors into the land of death?"

"I—" Abbas began, stepping back. He stiffened as Tuerto snorted. "Yes. Better a true servant of Allah than a moneygrubbing creature such as you," he snapped. "You only want the woman alive because you fancy her!"

"And so? I take my pleasures here, rather than in the afterlife. What business is that of yours?" Tuerto said, dropping his hands.

"It is my business when it is obvious that your pleasures have become a liability!" Abbas said, pulling his pistol. "And liabilities must be disposed of!"

"I agree," Tuerto said. His arm whipped forward in one smooth motion and a throwing blade sliced into Abbas's hand, causing him to drop his weapon with a squeal. Tuerto unholstered his own pistol and stepped forward. "Goodbye, Abbas, my friend." With barely a twitch of a smile, he shot Abbas in the head. The body toppled backward and landed on the floor with a heavy thump. Tuerto looked around the room at the other nine men. "Organize what remains of the Holy One Hundred. Get them ready to go. Those who can, will be leaving within the hour. Go. Now!"

His men filed out quickly, not a one of them looking at Abbas's corpse splayed out on the floor. Tuerto looked at the bed, and Tanzir. Leaning over, he patted her cheek. "You are welcome, little policewoman," he whispered before he turned and left. Closing and locking the door behind him, he wondered if he had made the right choice. In truth, he had been planning to kill Abbas sooner or later. The man had been an annoying pig. And the woman might prove useful, in one fashion or another.

Shaking his head, he started downstairs. Sweets was waiting for him, a shot glass spinning on the table in front of him. "You shoot him?" the coyote asked.

For a moment, Tuerto thought Sweets meant Abbas, and then he shook his head. "No. James still lives. He may wish otherwise soon enough, however." He picked up the shot glass and set it upright. "We will leave soon, I think."

"Groovy. Just need to renegotiate first," Sweets said, seemingly unconcerned about the shot he had heard. "Less men means more work and I lost four guys, counting Jorge."

"And I lost ten," Tuerto said. Then he corrected himself. "Eleven."

"More than that. Jorge killed two of 'em. And the broad sure as hell killed that poor bastard she lit up."

"There are plenty left," Tuerto said, shrugging.

"Still leaves eighty-odd boys for six trucks. No, excuse me, two vans." Sweets held up two fingers. "Cousin Frank busted up the trucks. And the fire fucked 'em up beyond repair. And them cheap-ass vans we got ain't going to make it over the border."

"You're sure?" Tuerto demanded.

"Yep," Sweets said. "We got two vehicles that can go-go gadget. Scarcity means prices go up. That's just simple economics."

"At this point, I wonder whether we should simply cut our losses," Tuerto said, rolling the shot glass around and around with one finger. He fixed Sweets with a contemplative eye. "If you cannot drive, you are not useful, Mr. Sweets."

"Use is relative," Sweets said calmly. "Any way you slice it, me and Digger are the most useful motherfuckers you got."

"And the others?"

"Screw 'em. But me and Digger can get gone ASAP, which is probably what you want about nowish." Sweets pulled a wireless radio up off the floor and set it on the table. "You speak Mexican?"

"I speak Spanish," Tuerto said.

"Right," Sweets said, baring his teeth in an ugly grin. "Give this a listen, if you would." He turned the radio on and spun the knob. Static settled into a babble of voices. Tuerto listened and then cursed. He recognized military jargon when he heard it, regardless of the language.

"Are you certain?"

"As certain as can be. The *Federales* are on the way. Someone tipped them off to this little operation, we knew that. But now somebody up north has goosed them into actually moving, and brother, they are hauling ass in our direction. Care to guess what that means?"

"They are waiting on us," Tuerto said quietly. He cursed again and the shot glass shattered as he hurled it across the room. He brought himself under control and looked upward, frowning. The noose was no longer just some ephemeral feeling, but instead a very physical threat. "We can still salvage this."

"Of course we can." Sweets leaned back and threw his boots up on the table, crossing them at the ankles. "As soon as we renegotiate, that is."

"And you believe that now is the time?" Tuerto said, somewhat impressed despite himself.

"When better, I ask you," Sweets said.

"Anytime other than now, ideally," Tuerto snapped, pinching the bridge of his nose.

"Nah, but I'm not greedy. Double, split between me and Digger," Sweets said, gesturing with his finger. "Easy-peasy-lemon-squeezy…we can get shed of this place before the *Federales* get here, and whoever is left behind, well, they'll provide one hell of a distraction, right?"

"Right," the mercenary said dubiously. He wasn't that enamored of his men that leaving them behind bothered him, but he didn't trust Sweets further than he could throw him. "What about the others? What about our would-be immigrants?"

"Screw them, too," Sweets said cheerfully. "They ain't useful no more, not now that we've been made. Shoot them, burn 'em or let them go. I couldn't give two shits."

Tuerto sat back, considering. His paymasters wouldn't be happy if he failed, and he could do without being hunted by vengeful terrorists who thought he'd taken their money and run. And Sweets and his brother would be easy enough to dispose of, when they inevitably got too frisky and tried something.

"Fine. Double the original fee, split between you and your brother," Tuerto said.

"And the woman," Sweets added.

"What?"

"The woman," Sweets said. "You might think you need her for a hostage, but Digger needs her more. And you need Digger more than you need her." He smiled. "Give him to her, and he'll take you wherever you need to go."

Tuerto frowned and drummed his fingers on the tabletop. He'd killed one of his own men to preserve her life. Could he just hand her over to a fiend like Digger? He grunted. Of course he could. In the end, his own life was more important.

"As you wish, but we must leave now," he said.

"Oh, definitely," Sweets said. "With two vehicles we can get half your boys easy across the border, barring any more mishaps." Sweets knocked on the table. "Knock on wood."

The brisk *crack-crack-crack* of an assault rifle caused both men to leap to their feet. Tuerto glared at Sweets. "You had to say that," he said.

20

Bolan moved through the desert like a shadow, his rangy frame gliding through the purple light. The sun was setting in a silent explosion of color, but the Executioner had no time for beauty, nor for the chill that was creeping into the air. He carried a modified H&K, similar to the one he'd lost, and a new Desert Eagle rested on his hip, plus a replacement KA-BAR. The weapons were familiar, and knowing Kissinger had sent them meant that Bolan could rely on them implicitly.

The helicopter had set him down a mile or so away from the town, and he moved quickly despite the strain that he still felt down deep in his limbs and joints. Pain could be pushed aside if the situation was desperate enough, and if this situation weren't desperate, Bolan didn't know what would qualify.

The rest he'd been able to grab had done him a world of good, giving his impressive constitution some much-needed time to recharge. Getting closer to his destination, Bolan dropped low and crawled through a maze of saguaros and scrub bushes. The town was much as he remembered, though presently there were columns of smoke rising up into the swiftly darkening sky.

Someone had been having fun, it seemed. And Bolan figured that the smoke was a good omen…if there was ever a sign that James was alive, that was it. Grinning like a wolf, Bolan slithered forward and crept toward the outskirts of the town.

As he got closer he saw that it was abuzz with activity. Men were hurrying back and forth, yelling. Bolan stopped and sank down, thinking. They must know that the *Federales* were on their way, somehow. That meant they'd be on their guard. It also meant that they wouldn't be looking for one man.

It took him ten more minutes to get into town. Flat against a clapboard wall, he peered around a corner, judging the terrain. He could smell burning oil and rubber. His eyes found the building where the illegal immigrants were being held. Three men were heading for it, their weapons held purposefully. Bolan knew their intentions. If they were aware that their cover was blown, then there was no further need for those people in there.

The debate lasted only moments. Bolan had a duty, and he would not shirk it. As quiet as a panther, he shadowed the trio, gently taking the safety off of his H&K. It had a noise suppressor attached, and hopefully, any shots the terrorists got off would be misconstrued as being an execution under way.

One of them bent to unlock the padlock as the other two readied their assault rifles. Bolan sprang into action without an iota of hesitation to mar the smoothness of his movement. The KA-BAR swept out, cutting across the back of one man's neck, slicing through his spinal column and nearly decapitating him. He fell without a sound, toppling forward. The other turned, his face going pale. Bolan shot him, the H&K making a quiet "chuff" of sound. The third man jerked to his feet, reaching for the weapon slung over his back. He opened his mouth to yell and Bolan, thinking quickly, jammed the blade of his knife through the man's open mouth, nailing him to the door. The man gurgled, and Bolan shot him in the chest, putting him out of his misery. He jerked the blade free, letting the body fall.

Bolan shot the lock off and opened the door. A number of frightened faces met his and he held up a hand. "It's okay," he said in Spanish. "I'm not here to hurt you."

They didn't seem to believe him, but he couldn't help that.

They had no reason to trust a man with a gun, no matter how friendly he seemed. As far as they were concerned, he might just as well have been a cartel soldier as a rescuer.

"Is there an Amira Tanzir here?" Bolàn said, speaking over the rising tide of whispers. "Amira Tanzir?"

"She was taken," someone said. It was an older woman who was heavyset and tired and scared looking. Bolan could practically smell the stink of tension and fear on the close air of the former dance hall. "She set the fires, tried to escape. They took her," she went on, shaking her head. "She shouldn't have tried to run."

"She didn't," Bolan said. "You all need to leave. Things are about to become very loud and very dangerous around here." He lifted his weapon meaningfully.

"Where will we go?" the woman said. Apparently she had assumed the spokeswoman role for the crowd. "We are in the middle of nowhere, and we have barely had any water or food for the past three days."

Bolan grimaced. He had expected as much, but he wasn't happy about it. Thinking quickly, he stepped outside and dragged the three bodies inside. Several people murmured in protest, but Bolan ignored them.

"Take these weapons and barricade the doors. When the *Federales* arrive, surrender quickly," Bolan said, checking the weapons and then handing them off. "They are aware that you're here, so don't worry. But until they come knocking, keep your heads down and the doors closed."

"And then what?" the woman said, hefting one of the assault rifles with a disturbing air of familiarity. For a moment, Bolan wondered what her story was, and how she had ended up here. Then his mind turned back to the business at hand.

"And then you go home. Maybe you try again later. Maybe not," Bolan said. "But this time, you go home."

"The cartels will not be happy," the woman said. "They will kill us."

"No," Bolan said, "They won't. I swear it."

"What can you do?" she said, eyeing him frankly. "Our government cannot stop them, any more than they can stop these men." She kicked one of the bodies.

Bolan hefted his submachine gun. "I am not a government. And I will kill them." And he knew that he would, if he survived this. The irony of calling what he did a war was not lost on Bolan, even at moments like this. Wars ended. But for the Executioner, there was always someone else to fight. There was always someone else who needed to be taken down, so that the innocent might live.

"I think maybe you will," she said, nodding. Bolan stepped back outside and closed the doors, scuffing dirt over the bloodstains as he went. There was no reason to draw attention to himself before it was necessary.

He padded on, avoiding confrontation. Bolan had more experience than most in slinking through enemy territory without being detected, and it served him well in the narrow, dusty streets. Soon enough, the familiar hulk of the old saloon beckoned him, and he thought about what James had told him about Sweets and about his cowboy fixation. In retrospect, it seemed obvious. Where else would a man like Sweets choose to make his headquarters?

Staying out of sight of the men at the front, Bolan made his way to the rear of the building and entered the alleyway that separated it from the next building over. The space was narrow enough that he could use it to his advantage, and he did so at once, pressing one foot and one palm to each wall, he spider-crawled up, pushing himself toward the top-story windows.

He muttered a silent prayer, hoping the rooms they opened onto were empty or, at the very least, no one stuck their heads out while he was in such a precarious position. The burns on his shoulders and chest pulled and wept beneath his combat vest, and he bit back a hiss of pain. Slapping into the windowsill, he grabbed it with both hands and hauled himself through the glassless frame, into the room.

No one was inside, and the room was barren of everything save a thick layer of dust and grime. He crept to the door and listened, hearing nothing. Then he opened it a crack and peered through. The corridor beyond was empty. He closed the door and crouched, weighing the odds. If James and Tanzir were still alive, they were in this building. Sweets and Tuerto would have no reason to move them, unless they had decided to do to them what they had done to Bolan, and the Executioner doubted that. They were too valuable as bargaining chips, and they needed them in one piece.

He stood and opened the door, stepping out, his weapon held ready. He moved close to the door across the hall and listened. Movement; he counted in his head. One, two…three!

Bolan kicked open the door and fired three times, blasting the two *mujahedeen* and dropping them like stones. Letting the gun dangle, he unsheathed his knife and cut the bonds holding James to the bed. The young man looked like death warmed over. He gave a weak smile as Bolan helped him to his feet. His wounds had been bandaged, but he'd lost a lot of blood, and he'd been beaten black and blue since Bolan had last seen him.

"What took you so long?" he rasped.

"Traffic was murder," Bolan said. "Can you stand?"

"I think I got my third wind," James said. Bolan leaned him against the door frame. Then he bent and scooped up one of the dead terrorist's assault rifles.

"Glad to hear it. I wasn't planning on carrying you out of here," Bolan said. He quickly peered around the corner of the door. Two men moved up the stairs at the end of the hall. One of them caught sight of him and yelled. Assault rifles chattered and Bolan jerked his head back as the air was filled with wooden splinters. He cursed. So much for the subtle approach.

"We could go out that way." James gestured toward the room's only window.

"I prefer the front door," Bolan said. Taking a breath, he stepped around the door and fired as he hurled himself at the door opposite. Crashing through it, he rose and looked around. As he'd hoped, this room and the next, closest to the stairs, were connected by a door. Without slowing, he hit it at a run, stifling a groan as the wound on his neck began to weep from the exertion. He surprised one of the gunmen, and cut the startled man near in half. As he fell, the *mujahedeen's* rifle chopped into the ceiling, sprinkling the floor with plaster. Bolan leaped over him and rammed the butt of his gun into the surprised features of the second man as he ran into the room to check on his companion. He fell, his face a mask of red. Bolan stepped over them and glanced down the stairs.

He emptied the clip at the men coming up, not bothering to aim. They fell back, yelling in outrage. Bolan lowered himself flat and squirmed across the landing, dragging one of the other rifles with him. "James, can you make it up here?" he shouted without turning around. Lowering his head, he swept the bar below with a steady eye. They had flipped over tables for cover and there were men scurrying in and out of the open doors. For the moment, Bolan had control of the situation. At least until someone thought to use a grenade. He needed an edge.

As if in answer to his prayers, the combat vest he'd lost earlier flopped down onto the floor next to him. James crawled slowly up next to him and grinned weakly. "Found it in that room you busted into. They got all our gear stored in there. Including everything they found in my van."

Bolan hauled the vest up and plucked the remaining grenades from the harness. Two smoke canisters and a standard-issue fragmentation "room-buster". He set them back and slid aside. "Have you still got that rifle I gave you?" James nodded yes. "Good. Keep a watch on our friends downstairs."

"Think they'll rush us?" James coughed.

"If they look as if they're thinking about it, pop one of the smokers. It'll buy us some time," Bolan said, tapping one of the smoke canisters. "Save the other one. And don't use the grenade unless it's absolutely necessary."

"And what are you going to be doing while I'm reenacting Custer's Last Stand?" James said.

"Finding Agent Tanzir and getting us out of here before everything goes to hell." Bolan eased himself backward and allowed James to take his place. When he was out of sight of the gunmen downstairs, he rose to his feet and moved down the hall, sliding the combat vest on as he went. There were two rooms he hadn't checked, and he found that the second was locked. After rattling the knob, he stood back and gave the door a kick. He didn't hesitate—if someone was inside, they'd have likely come running at the first sound of gunfire.

The first thing Bolan noticed was that the bed was empty. The second was the body on the floor. And the third was the rough bite of the nylon rope as it settled around his throat. Reacting instinctively, he threw himself back, catching his attacker between his own weight and the door frame. The rope went loose, not by much, but enough, and Bolan swept his knife out and up, slicing the rope in two with a twist of his wrist. He stumbled forward and turned as his attacker aimed a kick at his head. He caught an upswept ankle and threw them off balance.

"Is that a thank-you where you come from?" he said as Tanzir dropped back into a combat stance. Outside, he heard James fire off several rounds. He turned his attention back to the Interpol agent, risking an admiring glance. How she had freed herself, he could only guess.

"Thank you for what?" she said in slightly accented English. She lowered her fists and tapped fingers against the confiscated weapon poking up out of her trousers, its butt pressed against her belly. "Who are you?"

"Matt Cooper, U.S. Justice Department," Bolan said. "I'm here to get you out."

She rubbed her wrists. "I heard gunfire."

"We're preparing to make a strategic withdrawal to safety. Are you up for it?" Bolan said.

"We?" she said. "Is James—"

"He's alive, but hurt. We need to go, and fast," Bolan said.

"Where's Tuerto?" she said.

"Downstairs, most likely trying to figure out how to get upstairs," Bolan said.

"And where are we?"

"Upstairs, trying to figure out how to get down," Bolan replied. A thought occurred to him. "And I think I've got it. Follow me."

21

"Ol' Jorge has us pinned down but good. And no telling what Cousin Frank is up to," Sweets said, hunkering behind the bar with Tuerto. Every so often, a gun from upstairs would chatter and chop into the overturned tables or the wall or the bar, forcing everyone's head down.

"Cousin…? You mean Cooper? He's dead!" Tuerto snapped.

"Yeah? You check on that lately?" Sweets said. He tapped his head. "Who else is going to be doing this? And right now? You ever watch any Clint Eastwood movies? Guys like Cooper ain't dead unless you put a bullet between their eyes!" He laughed wildly. "Hell, he probably pulled himself back through the desert on his hands and knees, just looking for payback!"

"It doesn't matter who it is! The question is, what do we do about it?" Tuerto said.

"Could just burn this shit hole down, I suppose…unless you want to try to make a play for your sugar dumpling upstairs, Mr. One-Eye," Sweets said.

"We need to leave. Now," Tuerto snapped, not looking at Sweets. "All we are doing is wasting time!"

"Couldn't agree more myownself," Sweets said, tapping his cheek with his pistol barrel. "Triple then?"

"We already agreed on double!" Tuerto glared at him in shock.

"We got to keep on top of the changing situation, man!" Sweets said. "A van is already outside, engine running. Triple or nothing. To compensate Digger for the loss of his lady, if nothing else."

"I could just take the van..."

"And we could shoot each other to shit right here, save Cousin Frank or the *Federales* the trouble," Sweets said, aiming his pistol in a casual fashion. "Your choice."

"You make a persuasive argument, my friend," Tuerto said. "Cover me?"

"My pleasure," Sweets said. He shot to his feet with a wild scream and leaped over the bar, firing his pistol even as his boot heels touched wood. Moving swiftly, he began to back out of the bar, pulling the trigger as he went. Tuerto moved quickly for the door and out into the cool of the night, while all eyes were on the coyote. Quickly, the man with one eye snapped orders to those of his men who were closest and they fell in around him as he hurried toward the van with Sweets.

"What about the others?" one of the men, a wiry Saudi named Hassam, said. "Are we just to leave them?"

"Here or there, what matter where they give their lives, so long as it is for Allah?" Tuerto said. "We—"

The sound started off quietly, but as he stopped in midsentence, it began to grow louder. It was the dull *whop-whop-whop* of a helicopter. Helicopters, in fact. Tuerto's hands clenched. "We need to leave." No one argued. They all recognized the sound for what it was as well as what it meant. Their grand *jihad* was close to ending before it had even truly begun.

Sweets yanked open the back of the van and made a melodramatic gesture. "Load it up, son. Fill her up and we'll take her for a ride."

"Hassam, take these, make for the first assault point," Tuerto said, gesturing to the men around them. "If you do not hear from me in twenty-four hours, act as your conscience dictates."

"The plan—?" Hassam began.

"The plan evolves," Tuerto said. "'Be like water.'"

Sweets snorted. "Arabs quoting Bruce Lee. Will wonders never cease?"

"Good taste in film is universal," Tuerto said. He pointed at Sweets. "Hassam knows where to go. What he does not know, however, is the numbers for the account that contains your money. That stays here," he continued, gesturing to himself.

"What, you don't trust me?"

"Should I?" Tuerto said bluntly.

"Good point," Sweets said, grinning ruefully. "Where are you going?"

"With your brother," Tuerto said. Spotlights suddenly swept down from overhead, and voices speaking in Spanish echoed from loudspeakers. There was a rattle of gunfire not far away. Tuerto frowned. "I will see to a proper distraction and gather another group. We may yet salvage something from this mess."

"Digger's van is around back," Sweets said, climbing into his vehicle. He slammed the door. "Don't be late now… I can't refund them plane tickets to Barbados."

The van shot forward even as Hassam pulled the back doors closed. Tuerto watched it for a moment, and then turned and began grabbing men as they ran past. Orders spilled from Tuerto's lips with a fluency born of a hundred desperate situations, and he knew the men he had brought would fight and die as well as any. Even better, they would buy him the time he needed to get away.

Plans within plans spun in the mercenary's head. He was an expert at adapting on the fly, but this situation was rapidly moving out of his comfort zone. The original plan, to move north with the money, was still in play. But the distraction of the Holy One Hundred's attacks was looking less and less like a done deal. He cast a covert glance at the men around him. Who had seen his face? It was a substantial list—these men, the drivers, the Interpol woman and the two federal agents.

If they all happened to die, he could simply disappear. But he had to make sure. Easy enough with the Holy One Hundred; they wanted to die, and he was happy to oblige. As for the others… "Find the surviving drivers, save for the one called Digger, and send them to paradise," he said to one of his men. "No loose ends, brothers," he said out loud. "Kill the others, as well, those pathetic pilgrims looking to clean toilets in America. Send them all to Allah's grace."

The woman was the key. Taking a hostage was a risky thing, but the dividends could be lucrative. Interpol was squeamish about losing agents. If worse came to worst, he could bargain her life for his.

Yes, the woman was the key. He needed to get her.

BOLAN CLUNG TO THE WINDOW FRAME by his fingertips and tried to ignore the ache in his muscles. Tanzir, in contrast, was shimmying down the rusty drainpipe as if it was second nature. She dropped lightly to the street and pressed herself against the wall as she waited impatiently for Bolan to join her.

He dropped to the ground with a grunt, his knees bent and arms extended. Stretching slightly, he looked around. "Right on time," he said. Gunfire chopped the silence of the night into rags and tatters, and the growl of engines shouldered through the gaps. It sounded as if the *Federales* were getting their teeth into Tuerto's men, but the latter weren't exactly giving up.

A helicopter swooped overhead and he realized that the Mexicans were no longer the only players in the game. A sense of relief, slight but welcome, flooded Bolan. They might actually pull this off.

"What is going on? What is happening?" Tanzir said, wide-eyed.

"The plan got changed. I was hoping we'd have you and James out of town before this happened, but no such luck. There's nothing for it but to keep our heads down and make a break for it after we get James out."

Tanzir pulled her pistol and checked the clip. "Tuerto's men will scatter like roaches if this goes on for too long. And he'll be the first. We need to find him, and now." She slapped the clip home and started to push away from the wall. Bolan snagged her arm.

"First we rescue James. Then we'll go after Tuerto," he said.

"Not acceptable," Tanzir said, shaking his grip off. "Taking Tuerto down is more important than—" She bit down on the last part of the sentence before it could escape her lips, but Bolan knew well enough what she'd been about to say. It was a sentiment that he himself had once shared, more or less. He met her eyes, saying nothing. A muscle in her jaw bobbed and then she was moving away. He didn't try to stop her.

Instead, he sidled around the edge of the saloon, Beretta held low. Men were spilling out of the building as others readied glass bottles stuffed with rags. They were planning to burn the place down, probably more to destroy any evidence of what they were up to than to flush out James. Six men, the others were already scattering.

Bolan stepped out from around the edge of the building as the first Molotov cocktail tumbled through the open doorway. He raised the Beretta, took a breath and squeezed the trigger. Three men collapsed in the sudden blaze of firelight. Two more cocktails hit the windows and porch, scattering serpentine trails of burning alcohol and gasoline. The smell hit Bolan a moment before he went low and ducked behind one of the crippled trucks. He shot a running figure, causing it to tumble face-first into the dust and then the Executioner was up and moving around the back end of the truck, the Beretta bucking in his grip.

Two bodies bent and slumped and Bolan stepped over them and up onto the burning porch. Smoke invaded his sinuses as heat scorched his lungs and skin. His instincts screamed at him to back away from the flames.

Bolan stepped back and turned, quickly stripping the shirt off of one of the dead men. Tearing it into strips he wrapped it around his head and hands and then moved back up the steps.

Black smoke billowed out the doorway and shattered windows as fire spread quickly through the old structure.

Steeling himself, the Executioner plunged into the inferno. Fire caressed him with delicate pain as he raced through it as fast as he dared, and smoke pried at his sinuses, seeking to fill his lungs. Through tear-filled eyes, he caught sight of Agent James, collapsed on the steps. Bolan struggled up the stairs. He pitched back against the wall as a burning timber slammed down, taking out the banister. The badly made stairs shifted, creaking beneath his weight. Bolan jumped as they crumpled beneath him, his hands grabbing onto the landing, barely in time. He clawed wildly at the wood as his weight carried him backward and he dug strong fingers into the boards, pulling himself up beside James with a growl.

Swiftly, he pressed two bloody fingertips to James's neck and was relieved to find a pulse. It was thready, but there. Downstairs, a chunk of the ceiling gave way. What age and neglect couldn't do, the fire was, in spades. Bolan hefted the border agent in a fireman's carry and scrambled down the corridor toward the window. He had to get the man clear of the fire, and soon, if he was to make it.

The window at the end of the hallway was one of the few that still had a full pane of glass and Bolan swiftly punched it out with the butt of his H&K. Then, adrenaline and desperation delivering a boost to his strength, he kicked the rotten frame out of the wall, opening a hole wide enough for two men to go through.

Behind him, the flames crawled along the corridor, pulled toward the open air, crackling greedily. The whole building gave a shudder as it began to collapse. Bolan pulled James's hands over his shoulders and hurriedly stripped the sling from his gun, tossing the weapon aside with a flicker of regret. That was two weapons lost in as many days. It was getting to be a bad habit.

Using the sling, he lashed James's arms to his web gear and

tied them tight. Then, making sure the other man wouldn't shift loose, he swung out onto the outside wall and began to climb. Flames licked at his legs as he hauled them upward, arm over arm, toward the roof. It was a long shot, he knew, but James wouldn't survive a fall to the street below, not in the shape he was in.

On his back, the young man coughed. "Cooper?" he said.

"Right here, James, just hold on," Bolan said, sweat running down his grime-streaked face in sheets. His fingers felt as if they were broken and a spasm of pain rippled down the length of one arm. This would have been difficult even if he were in perfect condition. As it stood, there was a very good chance he'd carry them both straight to hell.

"Leave me, Cooper." James groaned, his weight shifting, nearly pulling Bolan off his perch.

"If you'd wanted me to do that, you should have said it while we were still inside," Bolan grunted. Something in his shoulder popped and he longed to give it a rest, but he knew there was no time. No time for anything but desperate measures.

His fingers found the edge of the roof a moment later and he hauled himself and James up over it as quickly as he could manage. The roof was already growing hot under his feet and he knew he only had minutes at most before it collapsed out from under them.

"Time to go, James," he said, looking up. He pulled a flare out from his combat harness and smacked it to life. Then he held it up as high as he could reach, hoping against hope that someone would see it in time over the glare cast by the flames.

22

"Idiots! What do you mean you burned it?" Tuerto howled, clubbing a man to the ground as his composure fled him momentarily. The others stepped back, staring at him uncertainly. Tuerto fought to regain control of himself. Fingertips pressed to his temples, he knew that it was unlikely that Cooper—if that was who was behind this—had left the woman tied up and that, as such, the burning of the saloon only made sense.

He could feel the noose tightening around his neck as his breath whistled in and out from between his clenched teeth. Never before had a plan of his failed so spectacularly. Never before had everything seemed to conspire so forcefully against him. It was as if Allah had turned his gaze aside.

Waving a hand, he forced his face into immobility. "Forgive me, Ali, I reacted badly," he said, stretching out a hand to the man he'd felled. "What's done is done. Our brothers give their lives to insure our success. We must move quickly."

Tuerto led them away from the orange light of the fire. Like the one from earlier in the day, it would spread quickly if not stopped. This time, however, it suited their purposes for the entire town to go up in flames and the sooner the better.

Every trace of them must be wiped away; every plan, every spent bullet. All of it must be gone. Only then could he be certain of survival, and of some measure of success.

The second van sat back behind a building, its engine already idling and protected from the aerial searchlights by the overhanging eaves of two rooftops. He grunted in relief. Something, at least, was going right.

"Where's the girl?" Digger rumbled, opening the passenger door for Tuerto. "I thought you were bringing her for me. Django said." Ali and the others climbed into the back, causing the van to shift on its wheels. "Where is she?"

"Back there," Tuerto said brusquely. "But we need to go, now!"

"Where's Django?"

"He has already left!" Tuerto said. "Go!"

"Not until Django tells me so!" Digger growled, glaring at the other man. "Not until I get what I want!"

"I say go," Tuerto said, pulling out his weapon and pressing it to Digger's temple. "Go, and go now." Digger gave a silent snarl and set the van into gear. It rolled out onto the street and the searchlights from the circling helicopters caught it, nearly blinding Tuerto. "Go! Go, go, go!" he shouted.

"Don't yell at me!" Digger snapped, stomping on the gas. The van lurched into motion, spitting sand, dirt and gravel beneath its wheels as it went. It sprang out into the street, nearly colliding with another vehicle. Tuerto swung his pistol toward the other vehicle, a military jeep, and shot the driver, a man wearing the uniform of the Mexican military. The jeep crashed into a building behind them as the van swept past.

"We have to get out of here," Tuerto said again. "Avoid the patrols. Can you do that?" he said, looking at Digger. "Or was your brother lying yet again?"

"Django doesn't lie!" Digger growled.

"Django does nothing but lie!" Tariq retorted. He turned back around. "Hey, look out!" he cried, grabbing for the wheel.

The woman had stepped out of nowhere, a pistol clasped in both hands. She stood in a relaxed shooter's stance, her face an iron mask of resolve. She fired rapidly and the windshield became a hurricane of glass. Digger and Tuerto yelled in unison and the former stomped on the gas, trying to run the woman down.

Tanzir dived aside as the van rumbled past. It turned sharply and one side rose off the ground as if the vehicle were attempting an awkward pirouette. Then, with a shriek of bending metal and breaking glass, it slammed down on its side. Tanzir rose from where she'd landed and hurried forward.

The back door of the van was kicked open and a man staggered out, the weapon in his hand kicking up a cloud of dust as he pulled the trigger. The Interpol agent pivoted and fired, raising a cloud of red from his skull. Even as he dropped, another man climbed out and took cover behind the open door of the van.

Tanzir hurled herself through a beckoning doorway as assault rifles spoke. Huddling in the doorway, she wondered if perhaps she should have waited for the man called Cooper to give her backup. Angrily, she brushed the thought aside. No, no, Tuerto was hers. Three years she had waited, and this night was the night.

With a snarl rippling across her lovely features, she stepped out of the doorway, firing toward the van. She shot through the windows on the door, knocking one of the survivors back. He screamed and tried to crawl away, clutching at himself. His companions wavered. The van caught fire a moment later and they broke, sprinting away.

She didn't lower her weapon. Instead she hurried toward the driver's compartment. The driver's side was pressed flat to the ground, and she could see nothing inside. The heat from the fire kept her from getting too close, but she saw that the passenger door was hanging like a broken limb, its bolt hinges split from the impact.

She cursed in frustration.

"Such language from so beautiful a woman," her quarry said.

She hit the ground and rolled as the pistol barked, bounding to her feet and firing in return. The man known as One-Eye staggered, giving a cough as his hand flew to his side. "Ah! Damnation," he grunted, firing again and sending her scrambling around the other side of the van.

Then, staggering, he began to run, leaving behind a trail of blood. After a moment, Tanzir looked up. She began to follow after him, blind to everything else but the path before her.

As the two of them moved away from the light of the fire, a broad hand punched through the remainder of the windshield. Thick fingers dug trenches in the dirt as Digger pulled himself out of the wreck, his face blistered and peppered with glass shards that glittered eerily in the light of the fire. He climbed to his feet, seemingly unconcerned about any hurts that he might have sustained.

In those last moments before the van had turned over, he had seen a flash of her dark wings. The black bird beneath the woman's skin was calling him on, filling him with eagerness. Digger flexed his fingers and swiped glass out of his bloody chest and neck.

"I'm coming," he said, following the sound of her wings.

23

The roar of the helicopter was as welcome a sound as Bolan had ever heard. It passed low and an emergency ladder was dropped. Bolan grabbed hold of James with one hand and the ladder with the other. Beneath their feet, the tar on the roof began to bubble from the heat of the fire below. The first lick of flame pierced the surface even as Bolan's feet left the roof and he was pulled up into the safety of the chopper.

Bolan set James into a seat and glanced at his rescuers. Carter, the FBI agent, nodded briskly to him. "Is this Greaves's guy?" he said without preamble.

"Agent Carter, say hello to Agent James, U.S. Border Patrol," Bolan said.

"You really did it," Carter said, shaking his head. "You Justice Department guys are hard-core."

"Just doing my job," Bolan said truthfully. "What's the situation?"

"We got one vehicle moving hell for leather north, but so far nobody has been able to break off and go after them. We got people en route to intercept, but..." He shrugged helplessly.

"What are we waiting for then?" Bolan said. Tuerto had to be in that one. Even if not, Bolan knew they couldn't let it slip away. If even one of Tuerto's men set foot on American soil, innocents would die. And *that* the Executioner could not allow.

"Maybe we should drop him off first, huh?" Carter said, gesturing to James.

James cracked an eye. "Fuck that. Go get 'em," he whispered.

Carter barked an order and the helicopter swung away from the town. Bolan checked on James, marveling at the amount of punishment the young man had taken. "You look like hell, James."

"Thanks, Cooper. That makes me feel a ton better," James said, closing his eyes.

"My pleasure," Bolan said, closing his own eyes, letting the cool night air wash over him. His skin was red in places, from the fire, and he stretched to keep his muscles from locking up. He had a feeling he was going to need every bit of agility before this night was through.

"What happened to Tanzir?" James asked. Bolan opened his eyes.

"She went after our one-eyed friend. I couldn't convince her to wait for help," he said.

"White whale, man. I'm telling you..." James chuckled harshly.

"Yes. I hope she does better than Ahab though," Bolan said.

The helicopter sped over the Sonoran Desert, swinging low and sending the wildlife, such as it was, running for the hills. The van appeared as the helicopter passed over a ridge. James blinked. "Is that my van?"

"That's your van," Bolan said, attaching a rappel line to his harness.

"That bastard stole my van!" James yelped, and then winced.

"He also kicked seven shades of crap out of you, but you're mad about the van?" Carter said wonderingly. "I take it back, Cooper. Border patrol is hard-core."

"He's tougher than me, I'll say that," Bolan said, tightening the cinch in the line.

"What are you doing?" Carter said, realizing for the first time what Bolan was doing.

"Getting James's van back," Bolan said.

"No way! We can stop them with the chopper!" Carter said, leaning past Bolan to bark a series of orders at the pilot. "There's no need for you to do this!"

The helicopter dropped toward the road and cut in front of the van, its rotors sending a cloud of dust flying up. The van turned sharply, veering off the road and into the desert proper. Carter cursed and the pilot followed obligingly. The back doors to the van flew open and gun barrels appeared. The pilot hauled back on the stick, pulling up sharply and nearly dumping Carter out the side. Bolan grabbed the back of his windbreaker and pulled him back inside. "You were saying?" Bolan said.

"Hell with it! Do what you want!" Carter said. His face was flushed red, though whether with anger or fear, Bolan couldn't tell.

"I always do," Bolan said. He stepped to the door. "Keep over them! I don't want to wind up splattered on the side of a saguaro somewhere!" he shouted to the pilot. The man gave him the thumbs-up and swooped over the van, keeping pace. Bolan took a breath and leaped. There was a heart-stopping lurch and then he slammed into the cold metal roof of the vehicle. With no time for niceties, he drew his knife and cut the cords connecting him to the helicopter.

A moment later, bullets chewed upward through the roof. Bolan rolled off, jamming his KA-BAR into the roof to keep himself from being flung off the bouncing, rocking van. He set his boots against the side of the vehicle and drew his Desert Eagle with his free hand. The big-bore pistol could easily penetrate the sheet-metal skin of the van and he wasted no time in stitching a line of bullet holes across the side. The van lurched and Bolan was forced to flatten himself against it as the spines of a cactus carved the back of his harness to rags and tatters.

When no more gunfire came from the back, Bolan holstered his pistol and slid along the side of the van toward the driver's-side door. Eyes caught sight of him in the side mirror, and a familiar grin beamed at him as Sweets ducked his head out the window and pointed his pistol at Bolan.

"Man, Cousin Frank! You're like a bad penny! We just can't get rid of you!" The Parabellum punctuated each word with a snarl and Bolan felt the burning passage of a bullet across his cheek.

Twisting with animal speed, Bolan reached out and grabbed the barrel of the pistol, bending it away. Sweets squawked and the van turned, whipping around a hundred and eighty degrees as he and Bolan struggled for the weapon. Spitting dust and blood, Bolan managed to wrestle it away and he let it drop into the night. He followed up with a punch to Sweets's face.

The van cut back the other way as Sweets slid to the side, shaking his head. Bolan grabbed the door and jammed his knife into the roof of the cab. Sweets lashed out with his boot, kicking the door open. Bolan swung out, clinging to the door with all his strength. Then Sweets slammed his boot against it to keep it from swinging back shut and howled like a coyote.

"Gonna scrape you off like a bug, boy!" he yowled, hands gripping the wheel with maniacal intensity.

Bolan gritted his teeth and reached for his pistol, hoping he could reach it before Sweets rammed him into a rock or cactus. He drew the Desert Eagle and it boomed solemnly, piercing the engine block of the van. The vehicle shuddered suddenly, like a heart-struck bull, and it slewed around and slowed.

"No! No, no, no, no!" Sweets shrieked, stomping ineffectually on the gas. Bolan dropped to the ground as the van careened forward; it was carried by its own momentum toward a saguaro that was at least twice its size. Sweets threw up his hands as the van crashed into the cactus and the top of the latter cracked and crashed down, perforating the cab. Sweets threw himself clear at the last minute.

He rose to his feet with a wet chuckle. Bolan stood some distance away, his pistol in hand. "You're done," the Executioner said, his voice like the bell of doom to Sweets's ears.

"Yeah? Well, it was a good run, right?" Sweets said, spreading his hands and stepping away from the van. He grinned wildly, his eyes shining coldly in the moonlight. He glanced up at the helicopter swinging around overhead and clucked his tongue. "I wonder if ol' Digger and Mr. One-Eye will make it? Probably so, seeing as how you wasted all this here time with me. And then, of course, ol' Philo will have his way with that little filly."

Bolan felt a chill course through him. "Where are they?"

"Who can say? Probably halfway to Tucson by now. Digger is a better driver than me." Sweets's hands dropped. "Always was." He looked at Bolan. "I always wondered what a last stand felt like." His smile spread and turned crooked. "Got to say, it ain't as much fun as them books make it out to be."

Bolan knew what was coming a moment before Sweets reached for the gun holstered at the small of his back. As the pistol sprang into view clenched in the other man's hand, Bolan fired.

Sweets sat down abruptly, his chest and belly suddenly soaked through with red. Legs spread, hands resting in his lap, he looked up at Bolan and said, "You…shithead." With a smile and a chuckle, Django Sweets toppled over face-first into the dust.

Bolan was already running for the helicopter, even as Sweets's body ceased twitching.

24

Tariq Ibn Tumart ran, his breath burning in his lungs. He ran through the ruins of his most audacious plan in years, and counted himself lucky that the bitch's bullet had only grazed his ribs. His pistol was slippery in his hand and he resisted the urge to look back.

He'd take his chances in the desert. He knew how to survive in the desert, though the Sonoran Desert was a world away from the sands of North Africa. He could live rough and lick his wounds for a few weeks, until they stopped looking for him. And then what?

The thought almost brought him up short. And then what? Back to Algeria? Al Qaeda wasn't going to be pleased. He'd gotten a hundred of their most fanatical men dead or in custody and not a single American death to show for it. That wasn't acceptable, by the ways that they measured things. He knew they'd hunt him down, no two ways there. He'd be dodging fanatics for years to come.

He could stop and surrender. Turn himself in to Interpol and trade information for a cushy life in some high-security detention center. He owed nothing to anyone, and struggle for its own sake was not a virtue he held dear.

He snarled in frustration. No! No, he could no more surrender than he could slink back home. He was caught in a trap of his own making, and there was nothing for it but to try to salvage something. Anything.

He would start again, with a new identity. They might suspect, but the services he provided were too valuable to be so easily dispensed with. They would forgive him when the Americans wiped out another cell, or the British killed another section head. Then they would need him. Yes, they would gladly welcome him back then. He rubbed his neck, still feeling the noose, despite the optimism.

He stopped as lights blinded him. Two military SUVs sat at the end of the street, headlights blazing. Men with guns and uniforms waited. Their tension was evident in their postures. Mexican *Federales,* looking for anyone trying to get out of town.

He realized that the sound of gunfire had died away to nothing. His men were either dead or had given up, their dedication to martyrdom waning in the face of an organized resistance. Killing a school full of children was far different from facing armed men, and many fanatics found their enthusiasm dimming in such situations. Such was to be expected. Not everyone wanted to die heroically. Tumart himself felt that it was far better to live to fight another day. Last stands were for madmen and movie heroes.

Tumart licked his lips. He was only going to get one shot at this. He stuffed his gun into the back of his denims and stumbled out into view, his hands raised. Men shouted at him to stop, but he continued to stumble forward, as if he didn't understand. His body tensed and then uncoiled. He threw himself flat and drew his pistol, firing. The headlights went out with a tinkle of broken glass and he rolled to his feet, firing at the last place he'd seen human forms. A man screamed and others shouted. Tumart rushed forward, circling around to the side of an SUV. Dropping to the ground again, he rolled beneath it and fired, plucking the legs out from under another man.

As the man fell screaming, Tumart slid out and shot him in the head. A third man raced around the end of the other car, indistinct in the darkness. The mercenary spun and fired smoothly, blowing him backward. Three men died in as many minutes. He took a breath and bent to see which one had the keys.

A pistol clicked behind him and he stopped. "Step away from them," Tanzir said.

Tumart raised his hands and stood. "Well, this is awkward, is it not?"

"No. You're under arrest," she said.

"Do you still enjoy saying that?" he said.

"More and more each time," she said. "Drop your pistol and kick it away. Now."

"Done," he said, doing as she said. "I surrender, of course."

"I have no doubt, seeing as you're caught." Tanzir stepped closer. "On your knees."

"Is this really necessary?" Tumart said, turning slightly. "I'm happy to go with you."

"On your knees, Tuerto!" she barked.

"No," Tumart said, whipping a throwing knife from the sleeve of his jacket and sending it flying toward her. She sprang back and the blade cut a red line across her chin. Tariq lunged for her, grabbing her weapon and trying to wrestle it out of her grip. "Give me that, witch!"

"Get off me!" she said, snapping a knee into his belly. He stumbled back, pain flaring in his side. She fired and he tumbled onto his back. She rose over him, aiming at him. "On your belly!"

"I'd rather not," he said. "Besides, you're out of ammunition." As she glanced at her gun, he kicked it out of her grip. Rising to his feet, he sent a blow winging toward her throat. She blocked it with both hands and they parted, breathing heavily. The sound of a helicopter rose in the distance.

"We could have been such friends," he said. "I had it all planned out. A trip across America, and then to Montreal. Lovely town, Montreal. From there, to Paris. The City of Light is wonderful this time of year."

"Shut up," she said.

"But you had to go and spoil it all by being an altogether different type of policewoman than you first claimed to be," he continued, ignoring her. "I am hurt, here, in my heart."

"I'll hurt you," she snapped, sliding forward, the heel of her palm striking out toward his face. He moved aside, and caught her under the arm with the edge of his hand. She staggered and he stooped, having maneuvered himself toward one of the dead men. Swiftly he pulled the pistol from the man's belt and aimed it at her. She stopped, her face going pale.

"It could have been lovely," he said.

"Lovely," someone said, behind him.

A noose of iron fingers closed around his throat and Tumart tried to howl as he was jerked into the air. He dropped the pistol and clawed at the fingertips exerting such inexorable pressure on his windpipe. His feet dangled several inches off the ground and the edges of his vision devolved into colored sparks and black smoke.

"Can you see the black bird?" a voice like stone grating on stone said mildly. "I want to know if men can see it. I want to see it, so you have to say. Can you see it?"

Tumart, panic washing away what remained of his self control, reached helplessly toward Tanzir, tongue bulging from between his lips as the life was strangled out of him.

"Can you see it?"

Tumart's vision went all black, and sound vanished, swallowed by the muffled quiet of oblivion. Inside his head, something popped and then Tariq Ibn Tumart, El Tuerto, escaped the final trap and plunged into whatever awaited him in the next life.

Digger shook the body, and then let it fall into a heap in front of him. "I don't think he saw it," he said, looking blankly at Tanzir for a moment. Then, slowly, a sickening smile spread across his glass-marred features. "You'll help me see it, though, won't you? I can see the feathers in your hair."

"I don't know what you're talking about," she said, realizing even as she said it that he was far past the point of sanity. Whatever thin blanket of normalcy his true self had been hiding under had been stripped away, and all that remained was a monster quite unlike the man he'd just casually strangled in front of her.

She felt no sympathy for Tumart's fate, but neither did she wish to join him in death at Digger's hands. Tanzir made a lunge for the pistol Tumart had dropped. Digger was faster. His hand closed on her wrists and he whipped her through the air, causing her to crash against the side of the nearest SUV. She dropped down, her ribs making odd movements inside her. She fell forward and tried to crawl away, but Digger followed her doggedly. He grabbed her ankles and dragged her away from the vehicle.

"You're being selfish," he said like a parent lecturing a child. "Django said you were mine, and I want you to help me see the black bird you've got inside you. All women have one, just like Momma. I need to see it again, just once. It was so beautiful and it hurts me in my head to think about it," he said, letting her leg drop and crouching over her. He drew the knife from his belt and pressed the tip to her cheek.

"I can't think of nothing else no more," he said, looking around at the burning buildings that surrounded them. The whole town was rapidly becoming an inferno, burning away as if it had never been. The fire was reflected in his eyes and Tanzir felt more frightened than she ever had before in her life. "I can't think of nothing but the black bird. I don't know where Django is…or anybody else. But it don't matter. All I need is you," he said, looking back down at her.

She kicked him in the balls. He squalled like a panther as she eeled out from under him and ran, clutching her ribs. Digger shook himself and loped after her.

She ran away from the fire and into the desert. The moon

beamed down with a yellow glare across the blue sand as she moved, her ribs grating against one another with every step.

The town was a line of fire when she stumbled into the gulley and crashed into the scrub brush. Breathing heavily, she tried to claw her way free. She heard rocks crack and pop beneath Digger's tread. And there was something else…a quiet, quick padding.

A shadow fell over her. Digger looked down at her. "Coyotes," he said. "They can smell them bodies cooking. It makes them hungry and greed makes them brave," he went on. "That's what my momma said." He gestured with the knife. "If you run, they'll take you."

"If I don't, you'll do the same," she said.

"Yes," he said, smiling. He reached for her as the coyotes in the darkness began to howl.

25

"Look, just wait a minute!" Agent Carter said as Bolan dropped onto the ground. "We'll get together a proper search party after we get James here to the medicos."

"No time," Bolan said, looking up at the FBI man. "If Sweets wasn't lying, then Tuerto is making a run for it."

"We've got the other choppers out now...they haven't seen anybody...no vehicles, no one on foot, nobody!" Carter said, his tie flapping in the updraft of the chopper's rotors. "They ain't going nowhere!"

"All the more reason to find them quick," Bolan said. "Agent Tanzir is good, but can she take on God knows how many men looking to die for the cause?"

"I—" Carter began. Then he shook his head. "I'll send backup. Interpol is on its way. Try not to get yourself killed, Cooper."

"I'll do my best," Bolan said as the helicopter lifted off and rose back into the night sky.

A moment later, Bolan was moving quickly through the heat and ash, his eyes scanning the streets for any sign of Tanzir. Carter assured him that the town had been emptied of everyone still breathing, including the people in the dance hall, but there had been no sign of Tanzir. Bolan stepped over a body and continued. Nearby, a building collapsed with a roar and cleansing flame caressed the dark sky. By morning, the coyote nest would be nothing but ash, and the plans of the Holy One Hundred with it.

But Bolan wouldn't be satisfied until he found Agent Tanzir. He hoped she was just holed up somewhere, with Tuerto in custody. But he had a feeling that that wasn't the case. When he found the second van, his suspicions were confirmed.

He stepped around it carefully, eyeing the dead men. Looking around, he began to put together a picture of what must have happened, and he was forced to shake his head in respect for Agent Tanzir. She was determined, he had to give her that. Then he saw the blood trail—both of them. One came from the side, and the other from the front of the wrecked van. Both of them were heading in the same direction.

He followed the trails through the town and came to the SUVs and the bodies. Bolan sank to his haunches beside Tuerto's body and he traced the marks on the mercenary's throat. Someone had strangled him, and crushed his windpipe in the bargain. Someone strong. A cold sensation settled in his stomach. Footprints made a strange pattern in the dirt, and he grunted. "Digger," he said.

It had been too much to hope that the big man had been killed. Bolan checked the clip on his Desert Eagle and looked at the desert. Somewhere, he heard the high-pitched howl of a coyote and his skin crawled. He broke into a sprint, following the footprints.

The moonlight cast a dull blue tint of everything, and he had no trouble following the trail. His heartbeat sped up, and he said a silent prayer that he would find Tanzir in time. This wasn't a race he could afford to lose. He pushed himself harder, running until his abused lungs flapped in his chest like deflated balloons and spots danced in front of his eyes. The smell of blood and a rank animal odor reached his nose. He slowed.

In a shallow gully, two figures struggled. Bolan drew his pistol and fired into the air, hoping to separate them.

Digger whirled, the moonlight turning his features into a

nightmare mask of blood and bruises. He bared his teeth and snapped like a wolf. Bolan recognized the knife in the big man's hand and he felt a flare of rage. It was his knife. A cold fury filled him as he contemplated just what purposes it might have been put to while in the hands of a maniac like Digger.

"Stay back!" Digger roared, jerking Tanzir up by her hair. She clawed ineffectually at his thick wrist. "Stay back or I'll kill her!"

"You'll kill her anyway," Bolan said, circling the brute. "If that knife even dips toward her, I'll put one between your eyes."

Digger's lips writhed, as if there was a logjam of words fighting to escape his mouth. "No!" he finally spat. "I have to see the black bird! Django promised and I've got to see it!"

"Django is dead," Bolan said.

Digger blinked. "What?" he said, his disbelief evident.

"He's dead. I killed him. But I don't have to kill you," Bolan said. "Give up, let the girl go, and we'll head back to town."

"No," Digger said, shaking his head. "I'd know if Django was dead. I'd know!"

"Believe me, he's dead," Bolan said bluntly. "Buzzard meat," he added. Out of the corner of his eye, he saw dim, dark shapes trot through the underbrush. Bushy tails wagged and tongues lolled. Coyotes. A dozen or more. They barked softly as they moved around, waiting. Bolan's skin crawled with a primitive dread as the animals looked at him, much as the jaguar had earlier. He'd been on the other end of the food chain more than once, and this night wouldn't be the last, but he didn't like it.

"Then he's dead," Digger said finally, the edge of Bolan's KA-BAR pressed to Tanzir's throat. "But I can still see the black bird. I can still see it if you let me!" he almost shrieked, the pitch of his voice startling the closest of the coyotes. The animals shifted, whining quietly.

Bolan's eyes flicked down, meeting those of the Interpol agent. She nodded slightly. Bolan fired high a second later, his bullet peeling a layer of skin off Digger's arm. The big man rocked back on his heels and Tanzir rose, jabbing her elbow into his gut. He bent double with a whoop and she climbed out of the gully as quickly as her bruised limbs could carry her. Bolan hurried toward her even as Digger made a grab for her. He fired again with the Desert Eagle, but missed. A second later, the big man had shoved past his former hostage and his arms circled Bolan like the coils of an anaconda.

Bolan was jerked from his feet and Digger squeezed. Bolan thrashed, trying to free his trapped gun hand. Digger pulled him close and his forehead cracked against Bolan's. With a cry, he tossed the Executioner to the ground and tried to stomp on him. Bolan rolled aside, his pistol lost. He pushed himself up onto all fours. Digger grabbed the ragged remains of his harness and hauled him up and slammed him down in a manner more befitting an ape or bear than a man.

All the air exploded out of Bolan's lungs in a rush and stars danced in front of his eyes. He was pulled up again a moment later and tossed bodily into the gully. "Do you see it yet?" Digger screamed, his voice a high-pitched animal screech. "Do you see the black bird? Tell me!"

Bolan shook his head, trying to clear it. A big foot caught him in the ribs, sending him tumbling. Another foot smashed down on his hand, and Bolan felt his knuckles pop. His hand went numb. He pushed himself up with his good hand and ducked under a wild punch. Coiling his legs beneath him he launched himself at Digger, tackling him onto his back.

Digger roared wordlessly and flung Bolan off him with berserk ease. The Executioner hit the ground hard and lay stunned for a moment, trying to figure out how he was going to beat a man who didn't seem to feel pain. With agonizing slowness, his myriad hurts beginning to catch up to him, he pushed himself to his feet just in time to meet Digger's rush. Bolan's good hand blocked a punch, and his bad one was battered aside in an explosion of pain. He kicked out and was rewarded with the pop of a kneecap shattering. Digger sank down, his fingers finding Bolan's throat even as his leg gave out.

"Tell me when you see it," the big man hissed, staring into Bolan's eyes. "Tell me!"

In reply, Bolan sank his fingers into Digger's face. The brute shook himself, trying to break Bolan's grip without losing his own. Bolan hooked the flesh around the other man's mouth and yanked as hard as he could. Digger screamed and reared away, clutching his mutilated face. Bolan rose and his fist caught Digger on the skull, knocking him flat. The big man rolled away limply, making no sound. Bolan stood and shook his hand. It ached abominably. It had been like punching granite. Only very rarely in his lifetime had the Executioner met an opponent so physically tough. He wondered what it would take to put the monster down permanently.

He felt eyes on him and looked up, expecting to see Tanzir. Coyotes met his surprised gaze with their own considering ones. There were more than he had first thought. Two dozen at least. What had Watts said back in Tapowo? That they could run in packs of up to fifty? This one wasn't that large, but it was big enough that Bolan felt naked without a weapon of some kind.

One of the animals whined. Another licked its lips. Bolan saw his Desert Eagle lying not far away. He bent, his eyes never leaving the gathered animals, and picked it up. The coyotes scattered abruptly, obviously recognizing the weapon. He breathed a quiet sigh. He hated the thought of having to shoot the creatures for merely doing what they needed to do to survive.

Behind him, rocks shifted. Bolan turned, swinging the pistol around and firing. Digger crashed into him like a bull elephant, driving Bolan against the hard-packed earth of the gully bank. His hands fastened on Bolan's skull and began to squeeze. Blind, Bolan fired again and again. Digger didn't release him, though his body bucked with every bullet.

Bolan dropped his gun and clawed at Digger's viselike grip. He had to get free, or he was dead, no ifs, ands or buts. Every sinew and ligament in Bolan's arms and shoulders thrummed like a piano string as he slowly, agonizingly, pried the man's fingers off his scalp.

Digger's face was flushed and sopping with blood and his eyes bounced in his sockets like chilies on a hot plate. His teeth champed, flinging spittle into Bolan's face. Bolan pulled Digger's arms away and held them taut, straining against the other man, muscle against muscle, strength against strength.

Then, abruptly, Digger's face assumed a confused expression. He let go of Bolan and reached back, as if to scratch an itch. Behind him, Bolan saw Tanzir step back. Digger fell onto his hands and knees, the KA-BAR rising like a gruesome fin from his back. He looked at Bolan with the dumb eyes of a dying animal. "I just wanted to see the black bird," he said almost sadly.

"I'll help," Bolan said, shooting him in the head. The big man collapsed, dead at last. Tanzir, limping, caught Bolan as he stumbled.

"What was that he said? Something about a bird?" she said.

"Nothing important," Bolan replied. "Thanks for the save."

"Simply repaying the favor, Agent Cooper," she said. "One police to another, yes?" Then, more seriously, "Can you walk?"

"If not, you have my permission to leave me. I promised someone I'd get you out of here safely. That includes not letting you get eaten by coyotes," Bolan said, leaning on her slightly. As he'd noticed in the saloon, she was surprisingly strong for a woman of her size. No wonder she'd been able to hold off Digger for as long as she had. Bolan wasn't easily impressed, but Tanzir made the list. She and James both, in fact.

"Promised…Eugene?" she said, looking slightly surprised.

"If by Eugene you mean a certain Agent Chantecoq, then yes," Bolan said, smiling tiredly. "He was concerned about you."

"Was he?" she said, as if savoring that prospect. Then, "You were right. I should have waited for help," she said as they helped one another climb out of the gully.

"I think you did okay, all things considered," Bolan said.

"I'll take that as a compliment," she said. "Was he dead?" she asked a moment later. "Tuerto, I mean."

"As a doornail," Bolan said. "Digger took care of him pretty thoroughly, I'm afraid."

"Good," she said. "In his own way, he was just as much a monster as that one, though not so obvious about it."

"Most dangerous kind of monster, in my experience," Bolan said.

She was silent for a minute. Then she looked at him. "How is Agent James?"

"He'll live," Bolan said.

"I'm glad," she said.

"I thought you might be," Bolan said. He looked up at the moon and then at the expanse of the desert around them. "It really is beautiful country, isn't it?"

Behind them, the coyotes began to gather around Digger's body. Bolan and Tanzir left them to it. Bolan didn't bother to look back. Nature cleaned up after its monsters when it could. And sometimes, it needed a bit of help.

Help that men like the Executioner were more than happy to provide.

* * * * *